Seven Days in Benevolence

Steven E. Wedel

**MoonHowler
Press**

Copyright © 2015 Steven E. Wedel

ISBN: 0692482040
ISBN-13: 978-0692482049

DEDICATION

This little book was written "on-the-clock" as everyone in my department at a major energy company was awaiting termination after our jobs were outsourced by the company that had bought us out. And so, the story is dedicated to everyone who has ever been screwed over by corporate greed.

ALSO BY STEVEN E. WEDEL

Novels and Novellas

Inheritance

Little Graveyard on the Prairie

The Prometheus Syndrome

After Obsession (with Carrie Jones)

Amara's Prayer

Collections

Darkscapes

Unholy Womb and Other Halloween Tales

The God of Discord and Other Weird Tales

The Werewolf Saga Series

Call to the Hunt

Murdered by Human Wolves

Shara

Ulrik

Nadia's Children

As Editor

Tails of the Pack

DAY ONE

Chapter 1

Dena Harris tapped the steering wheel of her Ford Escort in time with some unnoticed song on the radio. It was a Saturday morning and she was more interested in the screech of blue jays coming from the hedge to her left and the flaming head of a cardinal in the shrub to her right. She didn't know what kind of hedge or shrub they were. She didn't care. All she cared about was the big house that came with them.

She sat in the driveway of the house at 1009 South 12th Street in the small town of Benevolence in northeastern Oklahoma, waiting for the landlord to arrive. The house stood over her, blocking the morning sun so that she sat in comfortable shade within her car, the driver's side window rolled down to let in a spring breeze. The shrub where the cardinal sat grew at the corner of the porch near the steps. At the other end of the porch an inviting swing barely moved in the breeze. There were no curtains in the front windows; the Venetian blinds were pulled up so that the windows looked like blank, dull eyes. Dena resisted the urge to get out of the car and look through the windows. She'd done that twice already since first finding the house in the classified section of the newspaper.

She glanced in the rearview mirror and smoothed her red hair, more orange than the head of the cardinal, which had decided to leave the shrub. The car seat in the backseat of the car seemed very empty to Dena. She'd left her daughters, Brianna, eighteen months old, and Rebecca, age seven, with their grandmother for the day.

A Chevy pickup jumped the curb behind Dena's Escort and jerked to a stop in the front lawn of the house. A bald elf of a man hopped out and hurried around the truck toward her. Dena got out of her car and faced him.

"You're here to see the house?" The man pulled off his dark sunglasses and quickly looked her over. Dena noticed his eyes staying a moment longer on her legs than anywhere else. She'd worn the shorter of her two favorite skirts in hopes it would help.

"Yes," she said. "I'm Dena Harris. I spoke to you earlier."

"Dena. That's right," the man said. "My name's Harry Bosco. You ready to go inside?"

"Yes." Dena followed Bosco to the porch, where he flipped through some keys before finding the right one. He opened the door and waved her ahead of him.

The front door opened onto a large living room with three windows and two other doorways leading away from it. A black cable, like a thick, rigid snake poked from the floor near one wall. From the tip, Dena could tell the cable was for the television. Directly before the front door at the other end of the room was a brick fireplace. Beside the fireplace Dena could see the kitchen through a doorway.

"I just had all the carpets downstairs stretched," Bosco said. "I try to replace all my carpets every three to five years, but I have them stretched every time someone moves out."

"Oh. It looks good," Dena said, glancing again at the brownish-gray carpet.

"The two downstairs bedrooms and bath are through

here," Bosco said, leading her to the doorway on the south wall.

Dena looked quickly at the master bedroom. It had a ceiling fan and a small closet. The other downstairs bedroom was about the same, except smaller. The bathroom was small, but had an exhaust fan and plenty of light. The tub and sink were clean.

"The house used to be just those two bedrooms, the bath, living room and the kitchen here," Bosco said as he led her through the living room and into the kitchen. "The people who owned it before me built everything from the kitchen back and up. They also dug the basement. Then they decided to sell it."

"Why would they sell it after doing all that work?" Dena asked.

"I think he was transferred with his job," Bosco said. "All these appliances stay. Or I can take them out if you have your own."

"I'll need them," Dena said, looking at the mismatched stove, refrigerator and dishwasher. "They all work?"

"Oh yeah."

The kitchen wasn't very big, but it opened onto a big dining area with a huge picture window that looked out on a big back yard. The back yard was closed in with a tall wooden fence.

"Do you allow pets?" Dena asked.

"What do you have?"

"Well, I don't have anything right now," she said. "But with a big yard like that, I'm sure my girls would love to have a dog to play with."

"Outside dogs are fine," Bosco said. "Inside cats, too.

Inside dogs …" He shrugged. "I haven't had much luck with people who have inside dogs. The carpets never last long."

"I understand," Dena agreed.

"Here's your basement." Bosco opened a door under the stairway leading to the second story. "It's not a full basement, but it goes all the way under this back part of the house. The water heater and central heat and air unit are down there."

"That's fine," Dena said. "I'd rather see the upstairs."

"Sure." Bosco closed the basement door and led her up the narrow stairway to the second floor. It had the same carpeting as the downstairs area, with two good-sized rooms, one very small room and a bathroom that was twice the size of the one downstairs. Dena caught herself smiling in the wall-length bathroom mirror and forced herself to look skeptical.

"That's about it," Bosco said as he led her back down the stairs. "There's the detached garage, no automatic opener. Anything you want to ask?"

"Is the wiring and plumbing all up to date?" Dena asked.

"Yeah. As far as I know, everything works. I always come right out whenever there's a problem. If it's something I can't fix I get somebody else out. It doesn't pay to let things go because they'll only get worse."

"And you're wanting how much rent?"

"I've got it listed at $550."

"Uh-huh." Dena moved toward one of the windows in the living room and looked out, bending over slightly, just enough to make her skirt ride up her thighs an inch or so. She didn't like doing it; it made her feel cheap and kind of sleazy, but she needed to be frugal with her money. And, she admitted to herself, it wasn't a bad feeling to know that a man was looking at her after the way her marriage ended. "What about the neighbors?" she asked.

"Retired couple there where you're looking," Bosco said. Dena could see his reflection in the window. He was watching her backside intently. "I've only talked to the guy on the other side once. He keeps to himself. You probably won't see him much. Folks across the street seem okay. You got the field behind you. Nothing there but trees. It's a quiet neighborhood. A few kids, but no trouble."

"That's good," Dena said, straightening and turning back toward the man. She noted the blush on his face as he raised his eyes and found them locked with hers. "This is really more house than I need," she said. "Is your price firm?"

"Well, really, I can't come down too much," he said.

Dena bent over and scratched an imaginary itch just above her right ankle. She straightened and asked, "Could you rent it for $450 a month?"

"Oh, no, I can't go that low," Bosco said. "I could come down, say, $25."

"Umm. I don't know," Dena said. "I really hadn't planned to pay that much. I mean, it's a nice house, but I suppose the utility bills are pretty high. And cleaning it … It'll just be me and my girls, and they're both little. With two bathrooms to keep up, that's a lot more plumbing than I'm used to. I'd probably have to call you every time any little thing went wrong."

"You're not married, then?"

"No. Recently divorced," Dena said, giving a sad smile. "He found somebody else."

"What brings you to Benevolence?"

"I got a job here."

"I see. Where will you be working?"

"For the Main Street Authority, the downtown restoration project. As a secretary."

"Uh-huh. Well, could you go $500 in rent? That's really just enough for me to pay the mortgage payments on the place."

"It'll be tight, but yes, I think I can do that," Dena agreed. "Will you need a deposit?"

"I take a month's rent as deposit," Bosco said. "I trust you, though, so $400 will do just fine."

"That's so sweet of you," Dena said, wondering if she could talk him out of charging her any deposit at all, and deciding she probably couldn't. "Thank you."

"No problem."

"It won't get you in trouble with your wife, will it?"

"Oh, well, I handle the rental property. She'll never know unless I tell her." Bosco's head turned even redder.

"How soon can I move in?"

"As soon as you give me a check."

"I can do that right now," Dena said, pulling her checkbook from her purse."

Chapter 2

Saturday afternoon found Dena once again parking her car in the driveway of the house on 12th Street. This time her two daughters were in the car with her. She pulled all the way up the long driveway to stop in front of the garage door, which was at the rear of the house. Her mother pulled her Oldsmobile Delta 88 in behind the Escort.

"Is this it?" Rebecca asked. "Is this our new house?"

"Sure is," Dena answered.

"It's so big."

Dena glanced at her daughter and couldn't help but smile at Rebecca's wide, round blue eyes as she looked up at the second-story windows of the house. Rebecca's long blonde hair was tied off in doggy-ears and she had a faint red moustache created by cherry Kool-Aid. Only her little sister could rival her as the cutest girl in the world.

"Let's go inside," Dena said, throwing open her car door and stepping out. She stood up and turned to her mother. "Mom, you can't park there. The movers will need to pull up there."

"Where should I park?" Carroll Lentz asked.

"Put it in the street."

"In the street? But what if someone hits it?"

"No one will hit your car, Mom. Come on, before the movers get here." Dena watched her mother huff but get back into her boat of a car. Dena opened her back door and unbuckled Brianna from the car seat.

"Bye-bye?" Brianna asked.

"No, baby, we already went bye-bye," Dena answered. "We're home now." Dena straightened up, her youngest daughter in her arms, her oldest one already up the driveway before the steps to the front porch, waving for her to hurry. Dena smiled and went to join Rebecca.

"Welcome home, girls," Dena said as she turned the lock and pushed open the front door.

"Yea!" Rebecca squealed as she ran inside. "I wanna go upstairs." She raced toward the back of the house.

"It's so big," Carroll said, joining Dena and Brianna at the doorstep. "Why did you get such a big house?"

"There wasn't much to choose from, Mom. It was either this or a really trashed little house on the north side of town. This'll be nice."

"Can you afford this?"

"Yes. With what I'll be making, plus the alimony and child support, we'll be fine."

"It just doesn't seem right that Danny is paying you that money after you ran out on him."

"Please, Mom, don't go there. I told you that you don't know all the details to that. Just let it be."

"But Dena —"

"I won't discuss it with you," Dena said firmly. "Look, I appreciate you coming to help, but if you don't let that go, you might as well leave. I won't talk about it."

"All right, but I hope someday you'll tell me why you left your husband. I always liked him. I know your father didn't, but I always did." Carroll stepped past Dena and into the house. Dena rolled her eyes and followed.

"Do you want to look around, baby?" Dena asked Brianna as she put the toddler down. Brianna pointed at a patch of sunlight falling on the carpet through the window, jabbered baby-talk, then flopped down on the floor and pulled her dress over her head, cackling as the light warmed her stomach.

Dena gave her mother a quick tour of the downstairs, then gathered up Brianna and went upstairs. They found Rebecca in the largest of the upstairs bedrooms, looking out a window over the back yard.

"This is the room I want," Rebecca said.

"Then it's yours," Dena said. "Me and Bree here will take the downstairs rooms."

"I'll sleep upstairs by myself?" Rebecca's smile slipped away, replaced by a look of worry.

"You'll be fine. You'll have the whole upstairs to yourself," Dena said. "I'll probably be spending some time up here every evening for a while making curtains for all these windows. I'm going to turn that small bedroom into a sewing room," she said to her mother.

Just then they all heard the grumble of a truck engine and knew the college students had arrived in Dena's rented U-Haul with the little furniture she had taken from the home she'd shared with her husband in Enid, supplemented with a few spare pieces donated by her mother and an aunt. The two women and two girls went downstairs and spent the next couple of hours directing the unloading and unpacking of furniture, dishes and personal belongings.

When everything was unpacked, Dena looked around her new home. It seemed terribly under-stocked. The empty boxes took up much more space than her furnishings. Still, it was her own place and she was happy with it.

"We can put these boxes out tomorrow. I called a recycling company and they said they'd come and pick them up," Dena said. "I'll put up some pictures and it'll look nice."

"I'm sure it will," her mother agreed. "I should be getting home."

"Won't you stay and eat with us?" Dena asked. "I don't really want to cook, but I thought we could go out."

"No, you need to save your money," Carroll said. She kissed her granddaughters and left the house without a second glance back.

"I think I made Grandma mad at me," Dena said, ruffling Rebecca's hair.

"Why'd you do that?"

"Oh, sometimes she thinks I'm still a little girl. What do you say? Want to go to McDonald's?"

Rebecca jumped up and down, squealing. Brianna got in on the act, squatting low and straightening quickly, laughing and clapping her hands. Dena considered the matter settled, gathered her purse and keys, and the three of them left for a quick meal.

Steven E. Wedel

DAY TWO

Chapter 3

Dena awoke to the sound of crying. By the sound, she knew Brianna was standing up in her crib, her collection of pacifiers probably thrown on the floor. She glanced at the digital alarm clock and saw that it was just after midnight. Reluctantly, she threw the covers off and swung her legs over the side of the bed. She stood up, pulled her long nightshirt down to cover her underwear, and staggered the first few steps toward the sound of Brianna's crying.

When she bumped into a wall instead of passing through a doorway Dena remembered she was in a different house. That woke her up more. She brushed her hair back from her face and went down the short hallway past the bathroom to Brianna's door. She turned the knob – it squeaked a little – and opened the door a crack. Brianna had heard the sound and hurried around the inside of her crib to the door. When she saw her mommy, she held out both arms. Dena opened the door and lifted her daughter from the crib.

"What's the matter, Bree?" she cooed. "Is it those teeth again?" Brianna had been struggling to cut her cuspids for several weeks. The girl wrapped her arms around Dena's neck and put her head on her mother's shoulder.

Dena patted and rubbed her daughter's back for a few minutes, gently rocking back and forth as she did so. Brianna was still, so Dena tried to put her back into the crib. Brianna's grip around her mother's neck tightened and she began crying again.

"Oh honey, Mommy's tired," Dena moaned. Brianna continued to cling and cry. "Okay, okay," Dena said. She carried Brianna back to her bed, promising herself she'd put the toddler back in her own bed as soon as she went back to sleep.

In her mother's bed, Brianna snuggled against Dena, one short arm on Dena's shoulder, the sound of her mouth sucking her pacifier in Dena's ear. They both fell asleep.

"Mommy? Mommy?"

Slowly, Dena felt herself coming out of the blackness of sleep once more. She pulled her eyelids apart to find Rebecca standing beside the bed, her blonde hair standing out wildly, one fist rubbing an eye.

"What?" Dena asked, her voice a croak.

"My closet door won't stay open."

"So?"

"I want the closet light on, but the door won't stay open," Rebecca whined.

"Sweetie, can't you hold it open with a shoe or toy or something?"

"Okay."

"'Night," Dena said as she watched Rebecca slowly move away from the bed. The digital clock read 1:17 a.m. Brianna was pressed tightly against Dena's back. Dena scooted out of the covers, picked up her youngest daughter and carried her back to her crib.

Dena just got back under the blankets when Brianna began crying again.

"Oh, damn," she moaned, getting out of bed once more. She went back to Brianna's room. The room felt cold. Much colder than her own, Dena thought. She was too tired to bother checking the thermostat. She plucked Brianna from the crib and returned to her own bed. After a short time, Brianna settled down and went back to sleep. Dena drifted away again.

"Mommy? Mommy? Mommy? Mom. Mom!"

Dena sat up with a start. "What? What is it?" she asked, alarmed.

"My door's still closing," Rebecca said.

"What?"

"My door still won't stay open. I put a shoe in front of it, but the door closes anyway."

"Oh Becky ..." Dena rubbed at her face. She felt incredibly tired. "All right. Fine. You can sleep in here with us, but only for tonight."

Rebecca hurried around the foot of the queen bed and crawled in beside Brianna. She pulled the covers to her chin and was asleep within moments. Dena stared at the clock, watching the minutes pass until her eyelids drooped beyond lifting at 3:39 a.m.

Chapter 4

"You must not have gotten it in front of your door right," Dena said. She opened Rebecca's closet door and put the small white sneaker in front of it. "See? The shoe holds it open."

"But it didn't last night," Rebecca said. "Not for very long. It was open when I went to sleep, but when I woke up it was closed."

"Well, okay." Dena gave in, not seeing any point in arguing the matter. "Let's have some breakfast and finish putting things away, then we'll find a park and have some fun."

When they returned from the park, Dena put Brianna down for her afternoon nap while she and Rebecca carried all the empty moving boxes outside. They flattened every box and tied them in neat bundles at the curb for the recycling company pickup the next day. When they went inside, Brianna was crying. Dena hurried into the toddler's bedroom.

Brianna was sitting in her white crib, her red face streaked with tears and snot running from her nose. Dena knew she must have been crying for quite a while. She lifted her daughter from the crib and hugged her close, bouncing her and rubbing her back while talking to her. Brianna clung to her, her crying slowly going from a steady wail to hiccupping sobs and then silence. She became heavy and limp and Dena knew Brianna had gone back to sleep. She gently put her back into the crib and left the room, leaving the door open so she'd be able to hear Brianna's first stirrings when she woke up again.

"She sounded really mad," Rebecca said when Dena returned to the living room and plopped down on the couch.

"Oh yeah. She'd been crying for a while, I guess," Dena agreed. "When she wakes up again I'll set up the baby monitor so I can carry it around with me and keep an ear on her."

"When will they hook up the TV?"

"Tomorrow," Dena said. "I'll call them tomorrow morning and I'm sure they'll be out the same day."

"When will they hook up the phone?"

"I don't know. We're lucky the landlord kept the electric and plumbing turned on or we'd be in the dark and not able to flush the toilet."

"That's gross, Mom. Will you hook up my Nintendo now?"

Dena sighed. "Bored, huh? Okay, let's go."

They went upstairs and Dena connected the cables of the game to the small television she'd bought used for Rebecca to play her games. When she left the room, Rebecca was engrossed in a Mario Brothers quest. Dena went downstairs and put bags, water and ice in the tea maker, then returned to the living room. She ran through the radio stations and finally found a local one playing hits of the 1970s. As the old songs filled the room she began putting up brackets to hang pictures, avoiding the wall joining Brianna's room for the moment.

Evening came. Rebecca tried her no-school argument again.

"But Mom, there's only a month left," she

complained.

"That's a month of learning you need," Dena answered.

"I don't want to go to a new school."

"I'm sorry, Dena. I know this is hard. I'm sorry it turned out this way. If I could have waited until school was out for the summer to move, I would have done it. Things just didn't work out that way."

Pouting, Rebecca went upstairs to take her bath while Dena bathed Brianna in the downstairs tub. By the time the toddler was finished, Dena's shirt was soaked from the splashing, but they'd both laughed so much she didn't care. She found Rebecca sitting on the couch, her long blonde hair wet and uncombed. Dena put Brianna's diaper and pajamas on her, then turned her attention back to her older daughter.

"Want some ice cream before you go to bed?"

Rebecca's face brightened. "Yes."

"You brush out your hair and I'll dip the ice cream."

Dena had both her girls tucked into their beds by 9:30. She took a towel and went to the bathroom for a shower. She ran the water hot and it felt good pounding onto her shoulders and neck. She washed slowly, shampooed and applied conditioner to her hair, then simply stood under the steaming spray and enjoyed the sensation for a few minutes more before turning off the water.

Despite the humming exhaust fan in the ceiling, the small bathroom was filled with mist from the hot shower. Dena slid open the shower door and stepped from the tub. She froze, one foot still in the tub and one on the carpeted floor. For an instant she was sure she'd seen a human figure in the swirl of the mist. She blinked and it was gone.

She shook her head and looked again.

Nothing there, girl. You're just worked up about the new place. Stop it.

Dena smiled, but the hair on her arms and the back of her neck still stood on end. She thought the bathroom seemed awfully cold, which would account for all the steam caused by a hot shower in a cold room. She toweled off quickly and dressed in her pajamas, then went to bed to read for a while.

Dena was just about ready to put her book aside when Brianna woke up for the first time. Dena went to Brianna's bedroom, put the pacifier back in the baby's mouth, laid her down and rubbed her back until she was quiet again. Dena returned to her own bedroom to find Rebecca in the bed.

"What are you doing?" Dena asked.

"My closet door is closing again."

"Oh, Becky, come on. Did you do the shoe thing like I showed you."

"Yes."

"And it still closed?"

"Uh-huh."

"Let's go upstairs. I'll try to prop the door open."

Together, they went up the stairs to Rebecca's bedroom. Dena opened the closet door. Instead of using one of Rebecca's little sneakers, she put her daughter's pink Barbie Corvette in front of the door, with Barbie and Ken in the car.

"There, that should hold it open," Dena said. She went to the bed and tucked Rebecca under the covers again, kissing her on the forehead.

As she turned around to leave the room she saw the

closet door very slowly swinging closed, pushing the pink Corvette out of the way as it moved. Again, Dena felt her flesh breaking out in goosebumps.

"See Mommy? I told you it closes by itself," Rebecca said.

"Yes. I see," Dena said softly. "That's very weird. Hold on." She went across the hall to the small room where she'd set up her sewing machine and came back with the wooden chair she sat in to sew. She opened Rebecca's closet door again and put the chair in front of it.

"There," she said. "No wheels on the chair and it's heavier than your big ol' shoe, so it won't go anywhere."

"Thanks, Mom," Rebecca said as a huge yawn split her face.

"You're welcome. Now go to sleep."

Dena went back downstairs and got into her bed. She slept. At 11:12 p.m. she was awakened again by Brianna's crying. She spent an hour getting her toddler back to sleep. At 2:55 a.m. she awoke to find Rebecca beside her bed.

"My closet light burned out," she said. "And I think there's something in there. Something dead. It smells bad."

Dena only grunted, barely able to hold her eyelids up.

"Mommy? Can I sleep with you?"

"Oh Becky, we can't do this. We can't start this. I know it's a new house, but there's nothing in your closet and you're too old to need a nightlight, anyway. Please go back to bed."

"But Mom – "

"Becky, go on." Dena watched her daughter drag her feet out of the room, her own eyelids already fluttering. Her head fell back onto the pillow and she slept for a little more than an hour before Brianna woke up again.

"Damn house," Dena muttered as she brought Brianna back to bed with her.

DAY THREE

Chapter 5

Monday morning was hectic. Dena drove Rebecca to her new school, the first-grader complaining the whole way about how she shouldn't have to go to school. The amount of paperwork she had to fill out to transfer Rebecca into the school was double what Dena had anticipated. Finally, she had it all done and handed it back to the secretary, a tall, dumpy woman with a powdery set of jowls.

The secretary looked the paperwork over, smiled with crooked teeth, and said, "Good. We'll get her in Mrs. Witherspoon's class." She turned to Rebecca and asked, "Are you ready, sweetie?"

"I guess," the girl answered, her eyes moving from the secretary to her mother.

"It'll be fun," Dena said, bending down and kissing Rebecca's forehead.

"I'll show you where the room is," the secretary said. She turned back to Dena for a moment. "School lets out at 3:05."

"Thank you," Dena said. She shifted Brianna's weight, watched the plump secretary waddle down the hall holding Rebecca's hand until they turned a corner, then she left the school.

Dena visited three daycare centers next. She ruled out the first two quickly – in the cleaner of the two she saw a worker toss a toddler onto a cot and in the second she saw a gang of cockroaches scuttling across the tiled floor. The third was in an old Methodist church that had just entered the childcare business. Dena was impressed with the young woman in charge, Nancy Webster, and liked the staff members she met. The building smelled like old books and baking bread.

"Do you have a bus service, to pick up Rebecca from school," Dena asked.

"Oh yes," Nancy answered. "We pick up a few kids from grade schools. How old is your youngest here?" she asked, reaching out to tickle Brianna's stomach as the toddler clung to her mother.

"She's eighteen months."

"Really? We just got the okay to keep kids under two," Nancy said. "She'll be our youngest. We have a boy who's twenty months. His mom works at the bank. Is she potty trained at all?"

"No, we just started sort of working on it," Dena answered. "She sits on her chair before and after her bath and I try to put her on it when I know she's ready to do something, but so far we're not having a lot of luck."

"Well, she's so young," Nancy said. She mussed Brianna's hair. "You'll get it, though, won't you, angel?"

Brianna buried her face in Dena's shoulder and the two women laughed. Dena signed her daughters up and promised to see Nancy the next morning.

Her next stop was the Wal-Mart Supercenter, where she bought several yards of fabric, along with the usual household supplies and groceries. On the way home, she stopped at a Sonic drive-in for food. After she and Brianna ate corndogs and French fries, she put the baby down for a nap, measured the living room windows and took her bundles of fabric upstairs.

Dena flicked on the baby monitor and took the cover off her Singer sewing machine. She'd put the baby monitor transmitter right under the clock in Brianna's room without realizing it. A rhythmic tick ... tick ... tick filled her sewing room from the receiver. She could hear Brianna still talking and moving in her crib, but the sounds were relaxed. By the time Dena had her machine loaded with the proper thread Brianna had become quiet.

Dena cut the first piece of heavy beige cloth into wide strips, pinned the bottom hem of one piece and loaded it onto her machine to hem it. In short, throbbing blasts, the sewing machine drowned out the sound of the clock in Brianna's room. The first hem done, Dena pulled away what was beginning to look like a curtain and snipped the thread with a scissors. Brianna's clock ticked ... ticked ... ticked.

Dena pinned the top hem of her first curtain, making it smaller than the bottom and reminding herself to leave the sides open for the curtain rod to pass through it. She put the cloth on the sewing machine and reached for the wheel to start the needle. Her ears suddenly pricked up. Her hand froze an inch from the machine.

... tick ... tick ... tick ... tick ...

Dena put her fingers on the sewing machine wheel.

A soft crackling sound came from the baby monitor receiver. It lasted for about two seconds, then stopped. A few heartbeats later it was repeated, this time lasting just a little longer. Dena dismissed it.

Must be a radio station interfering with it. Or maybe an airplane.

She hemmed the top of her curtain. As she was measuring and pinning the bottom of her second piece of cloth, she paused and listened to the receiver again.

.... tick .... tick .... tick ....

She was sure the clock had slowed.

"I just put new batteries in that damn thing," she muttered, thinking of the pack of Energizers she'd opened the day before.

The receiver crackled with static again, this time louder. Dena gave it a suspicious look, loaded her fabric on the machine, and started the bobbing needle. She reached the end of her hem and stopped the machine.

.... tick .... tick .... tick ...

"Miiinnnnnne."

Dena left the room at a run, her feet barely touching the stairs as she flew to Brianna's closed bedroom door. She paused at the door, didn't hear anything, took a deep breath and opened the door as quietly as she could.

Brianna was sleeping deeply in her crib, her small red lips parted, her knees tucked beneath her and one pacifier held loosely in a pudgy hand. Dena looked to the white-and-blue baby monitor transmitter, then up to the clock, a timepiece her mother had made from a needlepoint kit. The face was decorated with a red kitten playing with a ball of yellow yarn. The second hand pointed straight down at the 6, futilely ticking as it tried unsuccessfully to move up the face, rising one second and falling back to the bottom, lacking the power to fulfill its function.

Dena took the round clock off its nail, looked all around Brianna's room one more time, then left, pulling the door closed behind her. Brianna never stirred. Dena turned the clock over and looked at the battery to make sure it was installed correctly. It was. She carried it to the dining room table, where she put in a fresh battery. She left the clock on the table to put back in her daughter's room later.

Reluctant to return to her sewing, Dena went to the front and back doors of the house, locking them and checking every window. Finally, she poured herself a glass of ice water, cast one more look at Brianna's closed bedroom door, and went back upstairs.

The room was quiet. She put down her glass of water and picked up the curtain she'd been working on.

Soft, snickering laughter rippled like polluted water from the baby monitor.

Dena ran back to Brianna's room. She saw nothing, but this time she scooped her daughter from the crib and sat in a rocking chair in the living room until Brianna woke up.

A radio signal? A cell phone? My tired imagination?

Dena didn't know what the explanation was for the laughter she thought she'd heard, but she couldn't get it out of her mind.

Chapter 6

"Mom, is our house haunted?" Rebecca asked as soon as she got into the car after school.

Dena felt the hair at the nape of her neck tingle just a little at the question. She glanced at her daughter quickly as she pushed the gearshift into first and eased away from the curb. "Of course not," she said. "How was your first day in the new school? Did you make some new friends?"

"They say bad things happened in our house and that we shouldn't live there. They say the ghosts'll get us."

"Who says that?"

"Everyone."

"Who?"

"Austin and Shelby and Christina and … everybody."

"Those are your new friends?"

"I guess so."

"Sounds like they're just trying to tease you," Dena said.

"Mrs. Witherspoon said bad things happened in our house, but it was a long time ago," Rebecca argued.

"Becky, bad things happen a lot of places. Just because – " Dena was interrupted by a wail from Brianna. She checked her rearview mirror for a look at the toddler. "Will you give your sister her pacifier. She's cranky. She didn't get much of a nap."

"Why not?" Rebecca asked as she put the pacifier into Brianna's mouth. The baby stopped crying and closed her eyes.

"Oh … she just didn't," Dena said. She pulled into their driveway and killed the engine. The windows stared blankly back at her and Dena couldn't remember if she'd left the blinds up or down when she left the house. She considered asking Rebecca what the kids and her teacher had said about the house, but didn't really want to continue the subject. Rebecca, however, wasn't ready to let it go.

"So, our house isn't haunted?"

"Hmmm? No. No, dumpling, it's not haunted," Dena answered.

"Then why does my closet door keep closing by itself?"

"Oh, who knows? Maybe the floor isn't level or the air from your ceiling vent closes it or there's a draft around a window in your room."

"Do you really think so?"

"Sure. No ghosts. Okay?"

"Okay."

An hour later, a man arrived from the telephone company. He was a thin man with a goatee and a surly attitude. He announced himself, took a ladder from his truck, did some work to a plastic box under the eaves at the back of the house, then checked for a dial tone in the house. He had put his ladder back on the truck and was getting in the cab when Dena rushed out to stop him.

"Sir, about the installation," she called. "Will the charge be on my first bill? Do I have to pay it all at once? And what's my phone number?"

"Didn't they tell you all that when you placed the order to have me come out here?" he asked, pausing with one leg already inside his white truck.

"No. They didn't." Dena felt her temper flaring and didn't care. "So why don't you do it?"

The man didn't answer, but picked up the metal clipboard he'd already tossed inside the truck. He thumbed through some pages, then tore one off and held it out to her. "Your number is there on the top. I think you can divide the installation payment in half, but you'll have to call the office on that. I just install the lines." He got into his truck, slammed the door and drove away.

"Asshole," Dena muttered. She took the bill and went back inside. She'd barely closed the door before the telephone began to ring.

"Somebody's calling," Rebecca squealed from her place on the couch. "Maybe it's Daddy."

Brianna picked up on her sister's excitement and began clapping and saying "Dada," over and over.

"I doubt it," Dena said. She crossed the room to the small desk she'd put by the phone jack. She picked up the receiver and placed it to her ear. Nothing. She looked at the receiver for a moment, then slowly replaced it.

"Who was it?" Rebecca asked.

"They hung up," Dena said.

"Can we call Daddy?"

"Not right now. Are you ready for supper?"

"When?"

"Maybe later," Dena said. She looked at the phone again. *I suppose I should call and tell him our new phone number. The court said I have to stay in contact.*

"Can we have McDonald's again?"

"Oh, dumpling, I don't know if I can eat McNuggets two nights in a row."

"Puh-leeeeeeeeeeeze!" Rebecca tilted her head and

batted her eyelids as her mouth split into the widest grin she could muster.

"Oh, all right, all right," Dena said, laughing.

The sky was beginning to darken when they returned from the fast food restaurant. Dena held Brianna by the hand while Rebecca held open the front door. Dena found the house key and inserted it into the lock. Inside, the phone began to ring. Hurriedly, Dena turned the key, released Brianna's hand and rushed inside, calling to Rebecca over her shoulder, "Bring your sister in."

She snatched up the phone. Nothing. Dena turned so her back was to her daughters. "Hello?" She waited. "Hello?" Nothing. She pushed the cut-off button on the phone. No dial tone. She tried again. Nothing. She pushed it several times. Finally, there was a click and the dial tone hummed in her ear. Dena bit her lower lip and put the receiver back in its cradle.

"Nobody there?" Rebecca asked.

Dena shook her head. She turned around and found both girls looking up at her with wide, innocent eyes.

"Can we call Daddy now?" Rebecca asked.

"After your bath. Okay?"

"Bath? Take a bath?" Brianna ran toward the closed door of the bathroom while her mother and sister laughed at her.

"She loves her bath," Rebecca said. She reached over and flicked the light switch on the living room wall. The light burst into the room and died.

Dena looked up at the light fixture. She sighed. "I'll get her in the tub, then you can watch her while I replace the bulb." She opened the bathroom door and hit the light switch. Again, the light flared, made a popping sound, and died. Dena pressed her lips together to hold in the expletive she didn't want to say in front of her kids. "Okay. I'll get the light bulbs now."

She went to the utility room and took two bulbs from the new package she'd bought earlier that day. She replaced the living room light first, then the bathroom. She began running the bathwater, then Rebecca called out, "Mom, this one's burned out, too." Dena went back to the living room and found Rebecca standing by the lamp on and end table beside the couch.

"All right. Will you help your sister?"

While Rebecca went to put Brianna in her bath, Dena retrieved another light bulb from the box, leaving only one new one remaining. She started back toward the living room. As she passed through the kitchen, the new bulb in the overhead light in the living room began to flicker. Then it winked out.

"Mom! The bathroom light went out," Rebecca cried.

"Dammit!" Dena kept her teeth clenched and her voice low. She looked at the new bulb in her hand, then put it carefully on the kitchen counter before going to the bathroom. "Okay, honey, will you wash her the best you can. I think there must be a wiring problem. I'll go get a flashlight, then I'll call the landlord."

"Okay, Mom," Rebecca answered. Dena thought she heard a nervous undertone to her daughter's voice, but she ignored it.

From a drawer under the linen closet in the hallway where she'd put loose pieces of hardware, Dena took out a blue plastic flashlight. She pushed up the white switch. The beam of light was weak and lasted only a moment before fading away. Dena dropped it back into the drawer. She hadn't bought any D cell batteries at the store.

"I'm going to have to get some candles," she called to the girls as she moved toward the kitchen.

She had a handful of decorative scented candles she'd accumulated as impersonal gifts over the years, plus a couple of leftover spooky Halloween candles. She lit half her supply and placed them around the living room, taking one to the bathroom with her. She took Brianna from the tub and dried her off.

"I'll leave this candle in here and you can go ahead and take your bath. Okay?"

Rebecca only nodded.

"What's the matter, dumpling?"

"It's getting dark. I'm scared."

"There's nothing to be scared of," Dena said. "I just don't want to use up all the light bulbs if there's a wiring problem that's going to keep burning them out. We'll just use candles tonight. We'll be like the pioneers. Except we have running water. Okay?" She smiled and gave her daughter a quick hug. "Okay?"

"Okay. Can I leave the door open?"

"If you want."

Dena took Brianna into the living room and gave her a board book to look at while she found the landlord's phone number. She called the number and listened to the phone on the other end ring and ring and ring without being answered. She hung up, looked at the business card again, and tried the hand-written cell phone number. Again, there was no answer. *There should be voicemail on the cell phone, even if there wasn't an answering machine on his landline.* Dena hung up.

"MOM!"

Dena raced to the bathroom. She found Rebecca cowering at the end of the tub behind the shower doors. Her eyes were fixed on the water between her and the drain with its rubber stopper.

"What? What is it?" Dena asked.

"It's moving!"

"What? What's moving?" Dena looked at the white stopper. Then she saw it. A ripple, fanning out from a small point, forming a triangle as it moved from the near end of the tub, through the water, like an invisible finger, toward Rebecca's crouching, naked body.

"Come here!" Dena yelled, lunging forward and grabbing Rebecca by the arms. She pulled her from the tub and half-carried, half-dragged her into the living room. Rebecca was sobbing and clinging to her, getting Dena's clothes wet.

"What was it, Mommy? What was it?" she begged.

Dena shook her head. "I ... I don't know," she said. "A water bug, maybe. It had to have been some kind of bug."

"I didn't see a bug."

"What else could it have been?" Dena's voice was shrill and she regretted the question even before Rebecca answered.

"It was the ghost. Mommy, it was the ghost."

"No, baby, no. It wasn't. It can't be."

"Why not?"

"It just isn't," Dena said, making her voice stern. "Okay? I'll get you a towel, then I want you to go upstairs and get your pajamas on. Understand?"

Her wet hair hanging in dripping mats around her face as she stood hunched over and trembling, Rebecca only nodded. Dena got the towel, helped dry her daughter and wrapped the towel around her before sending her to find her pajamas.

"Now, what are *you* doing?" she asked, turning her attention to Brianna, who had abandoned her book and was standing below the fireplace mantle, blowing up at one of the candles and cackling at the flickering flame. Dena scooped up the little girl and turned toward the couch, then stopped. Reluctantly, she turned back toward the bathroom. Candlelight still danced from the little room, reflected and made brighter by the mirrored door of the medicine cabinet. Dena pushed herself into the room, Brianna clutched to her chest.

The water in the tub was perfectly still. Slowly, Dena leaned over, Brianna still pressed against her. She put her hand into the water and took hold of the small metal ring on the drain stopper. She pulled. The water gurgled, then began draining out of the tub. Dena stood and watched until the bathtub was empty. Nothing moved in the water. There were no bugs left in the tub when the water was gone.

"Mommy?"

"Shit!" Dena jumped, banging her right shin violently against the toilet. She groaned and quickly put Brianna down.

"Sssssit!" The toddler said as she ran past Rebecca standing in the bathroom doorway.

"I'm sorry," Rebecca said. "Did I scare you?"

"I'm fine," Dena said. She sat on the toilet lid and rubbed her injured leg. "What do you want?"

"Can we call Daddy now?"

Chapter 7

With each pressed number, Dena hardened her resolve. *I will not give in to him. No matter what he says.* She punched the last digit and put the receiver to her ear.

Danny Wahl answered on the third ring. "Hello?"

"It's me," Dena said.

"Hi, Dena. How are you?"

"Fine."

"How're my girls. I mean … well, how are the girls?"

"They're fine. I just wanted to call and give you the phone number here. Don't plan to be calling all the time, though. Understand?"

"Dena – "

"Don't start with me."

"What's the number?"

Dena told him. "Rebecca wants to talk to you." She put the telephone into her daughter's outstretched hand.

"Daddy, Mom said 'shit'," Rebecca blurted. "Right in front of me and Bree."

"Rebecca!"

Rebecca ignored Dena, paused in her speech and giggled at something said on the other end. Dena listened as Rebecca talked to her father. The girl gave him far more details about her first day at school than she'd given to her mother. Dena learned that there was a rabbit, a hamster and a lizard living in cages in the classroom. Mrs. Witherspoon had a big freckle under one eye and the school music teacher sounded like a singing dog.

"And, Daddy, the kids and Mrs. Witherspoon say our new house is haunted," Rebecca said.

"Rebecca ..." Dena reached for the phone and Rebecca pretended she didn't notice.

"I think there's something in my closet, Daddy. And there was something in the bathtub with me, too."

"Give me the phone."

"Mommy says I have to give her the phone. Will you come see us, Daddy? Please?"

Dena pulled the phone away from Rebecca. The girl gave her a hurt look, crossed her arms over her chest and stomped off to the couch. She pulled Brianna up beside her and turned on the television.

"Hello?" Danny's voice came from the receiver.

"That's all nonsense," Dena said. "The kids were teasing her. The teacher did not say the house is haunted. Only that something bad happened here a long time ago."

"What kind of bad?"

"I don't know."

"How long ago?"

"I. Don't. Know."

"All right, Dena. All right. You're all okay?"

"Yes."

There was a long pause. "I miss you, Dena. All of you."

"The girls miss you, too."

"What about you?" Danny asked.

Dena cast a glance toward her daughters, then stepped into the kitchen and around the corner. "What would I miss, Danny? Tell me. Do you think I miss you never touching me? Do you think I miss knowing that when I make you touch me you're thinking about ... about ... you

42

know what you were thinking about. No, I don't miss that. I'll never miss that."

"Dena. I'm sorry. I want to try again. I want – "

"I know what you want. You made that plain enough. I can't live that way, Danny. I can't and I won't. And I'm telling you again, if you ever try to come between me and my girls, if you ever bother me, I'll tell everybody what it is you want. Do you think your CO would like that, Sergeant Wahl?"

"Dena, stop it. Just stop." His voice was becoming angry. "I can't help the way I am. I don't want to be this way. I want a family. I want a wife. But I can't help it."

"Good-bye, Danny." Dena stepped around the corner and hung up the phone. She did it harder than she'd meant to. She knew Rebecca was looking at her. Dena couldn't face her daughter's eyes. She went back to the kitchen, lit another candle, and rearranged dishes in the cupboard for thirty minutes while she calmed down.

"It's time for bed," she said, finally returning to the living room. Brianna was already sleeping, nestled against Rebecca's side, a pacifier hanging from her lips like a hoodlum's cigarette. Dena lifted the toddler and carried her to her crib. The small nightlight plugged into the wall was still burning, Dena noted. She put her daughter in her bed and covered her with a thin blanket, then returned to the living room.

"Can I sleep with you?" Rebecca asked.

"No. You need to start sleeping in your own bed. All night."

"But I'm scared."

"There's nothing to be scared of," Dena said. "Do I need to call your teacher and tell her not to be telling you those stories?"

"No."

"Then go on."

"But my closet light is burned out."

"Just leave the hall light on."

Rebecca's lower lip came out in a pout and she began to stomp away. Dena sighed and went after her, grabbing the light bulb she'd left on the kitchen counter as she passed. She put the new bulb in the socket in Rebecca's closet and turned it on. It stayed on. She propped the closet door firmly open, tucked Rebecca into bed, kissed her, and went downstairs.

Dena sat on the couch and stared vacantly at the television. She felt nervous about facing her first day on the new job. Soon, her eyelids were drooping. She turned off the television, blew out all but one candle and carried that one to her bedroom. She undressed and crawled into bed, blew out the candle, and went to sleep.

DAY FOUR

Chapter 8

Like a magnet pulling at a piece of steel, the screaming ripped Dena from her bed and, before she was conscious of moving at all, she was in Brianna's room, the baby clutched to her, clinging to her, her tear-stained face pressed to Dena's neck as she sobbed.

Slowly, swaying on her feet, Dena got her senses gathered and realized what had happened. A moment after understanding she was no longer in her bed, she knew that Brianna's crying hadn't been because she'd simply awakened. The toddler had been screaming in fear. Dena felt the hair on her arms rise. She looked around the room, which was lit only by the nightlight. There were shadows, but nothing moved. She listened. There was no sound other than Brianna's crying.

Dena's eyes went to the window that faced west. There was a sickly plant of some kind at the corner of the house. *Were its branches long enough to scrape against the window? Was there enough wind to do that?* Dena couldn't hear any scratching or any wind.

She also could not hear the ticking of the clock. She looked at it and saw in the dim light that the hands were stopped at midnight.

"It's okay, baby," she cooed, patting Brianna's back. "It's all right. You just had a dream." She leaned over the rail of the crib and snatched a pacifier. Brianna took it eagerly and put her head back on her mother's shoulder. Dena patted her a while longer, then moved to return her to her bed. Brianna grabbed her and began winding up to cry again.

"Oh, Bree, come on," Dena whined. "Mommy has to start a new job in the morning. Please go back to sleep."

The toddler made no response, but kept her grip on Dena's nightshirt. Setting her jaw, Dena pulled Brianna away from her and returned her to the crib. Brianna was howling before she ever touched the mattress. As soon as she was down she got to her knees and was pulling herself to her feet as Dena slipped from the room and closed the door behind her.

"You've got to start sleeping in your own bed," Dena said, her forehead pressed to the door while Brianna continued to cry. Reluctantly, Dena went to her own room and closed her bedroom door most of the way to muffle the crying. She got back into her bed, but couldn't sleep. "Please, baby, please. Just go to sleep," she whispered. The digital clock beside her bed read 12:09 a.m.

At 12:13, Brianna's crying changed. The pitch went from simply being mad about being left alone in her bed to a higher, scared tone. Dena had almost dozed off. She jerked awake, jumped from the bed and ran back to Brianna's door. She threw the door open and ran into the room.

A blackness fled from Brianna's crib as Dena entered the room. It was as if a thick but sheer drape of midnight was suddenly pulled in all directions until it ripped into hundreds of pieces and vanished. Brianna was lying on her back on the mattress, her eyes closed, her pacifier beside her head like a discarded bottle cap. She continued screaming.

Dena lunged forward, grabbed the baby and the

pacifier from the bed, and retreated back to her own bedroom. She paced at the foot of her bed, never taking her eyes from the doorway and the hall leading back to Brianna's room. The baby cried, but slowly her steady wails slackened to hitching sobs and, finally, silence. Dena continued pacing. And watching.

It was shadows. Shadows that moved when I opened the door. That's all it was. That's all it could have been.

She paced and watched. Brianna became limp and heavy. Dena cast another look at her bedroom door, then went around the bed and put Brianna under the covers. She went back around the bed and pulled back the blankets on her side. From the corner or her eye she saw a figure standing in the doorway of her bedroom. She jumped, a hand clapped to her mouth, but the scream died before it arrived, escaping as nothing more than a high-pitched grunt.

"Mommy, there's somebody in my closet," Rebecca said. She rubbed her eyes, apparently unaware of the fright she'd given her mother.

"There's nobody in your closet," Dena said. However, she noted that her own voice suddenly lacked conviction. "What makes you think there is?"

"I hear her talking to me."

"Oh, Rebecca ... " Dena sighed. "Who is she? What does she say?"

"I don't know. She says you don't love me."

"What? That's silly."

"Can I sleep with you?"

"Dumpling, I've already got your sister in here ... "

"Please? I'm scared."

Dena looked at the digital clock. It was 1:11 a.m. Her

alarm would be beeping in less than five hours. She gave up. "Okay, Rebecca, but this is the last night." She pulled Brianna to the middle of the bed, then made sure Rebecca was covered. Dena snuggled back into her pillow and was soon asleep.

Just over an hour later, Dena awoke to the sound of people arguing. Her eyelids fluttered open, but she couldn't hold them up. She felt incredibly tired. Her limbs were like lead and she could feel a hood of blackness trying to cover her vision from the back of her head. She told herself it was just the neighbors. She let sleep reclaim her.

BEEP ... BEEP ... BEEP ... BEEP ... BEE

Dena smashed the snooze button on the alarm clock and was asleep again before she could draw her hand back onto the bed. Nine minutes later the process was repeated. And again in another nine minutes. The fourth time the alarm sounded it was accompanied by Rebecca's voice.

"Mommy, turn it off," she said.

Dena forced her eyes open. It was 6:36 a.m. She rolled her head around to face Rebecca. The child was already sleeping again. Dena pushed feebly at the blankets covering her. She felt weak and unrested. Finally, she pushed a leg from under the covers and put a foot on the floor. With a great effort, she sat up and held her eyelids open. Dena forced herself from the bed, stood wobbling for a moment, then stumbled into the bathroom. She let the cold water run for a moment, then cupped her hands beneath the flow and splashed her face several times. The water felt good, but did little to wake her up. She dried her face and went into the kitchen to start the coffeemaker.

She dressed in a khaki skirt and plain red, short-sleeved blouse. Then she roused Rebecca and sent her up to her room to get dressed for school. The girl seemed to be having as much trouble waking up as Dena had. Next, Dena turned her attention to Brianna.

The toddler fought waking up. Dena stripped off Briann'a pajamas, changed her wet diaper and dressed her without the girl truly coming awake. Dena picked her up and took her to the kitchen. As she put her in the high chair and fastened down the tray, Brianna woke up enough to begin crying crankily, reaching for her mother as she did.

"Down," Brianna said between cries.

"No, baby, you need to eat. You've got a big day ahead of you," Dena said. "We both do."

Brianna continued to fuss and rub at her face while Dena poured herself a cup of coffee. She sipped it greedily, hoping the caffeine would work quickly as she scrambled half-a-dozen eggs and kept the toaster busy at the same time. Soon, Rebecca came back down the stairs and sat at the table. Dena put a plate of toast on the table, lifted off a piece and put it on Brianna's tray.

"The toaster works," Rebecca said.

"What?" Dena asked. "Of course ... " She remembered the lights. Slowly, she moved to the nearest light switch and flipped it. The overhead light in the kitchen came on. Dena went to the living room and tried one of those lights. It worked. She turned it off and returned to the dining room.

"Must have been a power failure and they got it fixed," she said. She put some eggs on Rebecca's plate and Brianna's tray. "Let's eat. We need to go."

"I'm tired," Rebecca complained.

"We're all tired, Dumpling," Dena said. "Nobody's

sleeping."

"There really was somebody in my closet. The light burned out again, too," Rebecca said.

"I heard some neighbors arguing last night after you came to bed with me," Dena said. "Maybe that's all you heard."

"She was using my name," Rebecca argued.

"All right, Rebecca. That's enough. Just eat, then go brush your teeth and get ready to go."

Twenty minutes later, Dena had both girls in the Escort. She dropped Rebecca off at the school and very reluctantly left Brianna in the arms of Nancy Webster, the Methodist daycare operator. She refused to look at the old brick church as she drove away from her baby girl, left in a daycare for the first time in her short life. Instead, Dena thought about her new job.

It was a short drive from the church to the Main Street Authority office downtown. She parked her car in the small area behind the building and entered through the back door. Greg Verden, her new boss, greeted her when she entered the main office area.

"Dena, good to see you," Greg called. He had been sitting on the corner of a desk, talking to another woman seated in a chair before a computer, but got up and approached Dena, his hand extended.

"Nice to be here," Dena said, taking the man's hand. Greg Verden was tall, dark and, Dena admitted, handsome. She guessed he had some Near Eastern or Mediterranean heritage, with dark curly hair, brown eyes and a nice smile that showed very white teeth.

"This is Susan McCombs," Greg said, motioning to the woman, who stood up and came to shake Dena's hand.

"You didn't get to meet her last time. Susan works for us part time. She's been doing what she can as a secretary, but her main job is researching and writing grant proposals."

"And I'm glad to see you," Susan said. She was a heavyset woman who appeared to be in her early forties, with frosted blonde hair and sparkling blue eyes.

"I asked Susan to come in all day today to show you the ropes," Greg said. "Not that there's a whole lot to learn just yet. Like I said during the interview, Benevolence has only just joined the Main Street program. But, with Susan here bringing in the grants and several businesses wanting to get in on the restoration, we'll soon be off and running."

"And that's why it'll be so good to have you here," Susan added. "Somebody has to keep all these records. He sure can't." She nodded toward the boss and winked at Susan. "You should have seen it. He was just stuffing papers into file cabinets, then complaining when he couldn't find anything. I've been trying to fix that mess for two weeks. It's not easy, just being here part-time, because he'll come along after I leave and mess things up again."

"All right, Susan, all right," Greg said, laughing. He turned to Dena. "Really, she's right. I'm not much good at organizing paper."

"I'll do my best to keep you organized," Dena said. Suddenly, her face split into a huge yawn. "Excuse me," she said, feeling her face turn scarlet.

"We're boring her already," Susan laughed.

"No, really, you're not," Dena said. "I just haven't been sleeping well the past couple of nights. My girls keep waking me up."

"You found a place in town, then?" Greg asked.

"Yes. Over on South Twelfth," Dena said. "Ten-oh-nine."

"Ten-oh-nine? On South Twelfth?" Susan asked. "The Astor house?"

"Astor? I don't know anything about that," Dena said. "But, that's my address. The house has a name? But it's just a house like most of the others around it."

"Those other houses are newer," Susan said. "The Astor house is one of the oldest houses in Benevolence. Matthew Astor built it before white people were supposed to be living anywhere around here. Of course, it's been remodeled and built onto. But it's still ... Well, it's still called the Astor house."

"And I suppose it's haunted," Greg chimed in.

"Some people say it is," Susan said.

Greg laughed and was about to say something more when the phone rang. Susan picked up the receiver and began talking. She glanced at Dena and Greg, then moved away from them to call up a record on the computer.

"You've never heard of the Astor house, then?" Dena asked.

"No. Remember, I've only been in town about a month, myself. I came here from Tulsa."

"From the office of the community college," Dena said. "I remember. I guess I just assumed you were from here first."

"Nope. Grew up in Tulsa. I'd never been here until three weeks before I got the job."

"Do you like it?"

"Well, it's a small town, with all that comes with that," Greg said. "Do your shopping early. After six in the evening and on Sundays you won't find anything open but

Wal-Mart. Except a couple of bars and the bowling alley. Do you like to bowl?"

"Sometimes."

Susan rejoined them. "That was the mayor. He'd heard rumors that the railroad was coming back to town."

Greg sighed. "Not yet," he said. "People expect instant results. We've only just contacted Amtrak about getting a stop here. And that'll be only if they run a line between Tulsa and Muskogee, which is really pretty doubtful."

"That's what I told him," Susan said. "I guess Sam Clayton was spouting off again in the Oklahoma City newspaper."

"That guy," Greg said, shaking his head. He turned to Dena. "Sam Clayton is a member of the State House of Representative, from Ponca City, I think. He's a big advocate of passenger rail service, which is admirable, but since Amtrak is subsidized with federal money, it isn't likely taxpayers will approve more rail service. Still, it would be nice to renovate the old Santa Fe train depot. The train service between Oklahoma City and Fort Worth has really helped all the towns along the line."

"I feel so overwhelmed already," Dena said. "You seem to know so much, and all I know how to do is type and file."

"Oh, that's all you need to do for now," Greg said. "You'll figure out soon enough what else is going on, then you'll be an even bigger help."

"Are you ready to get started?" Susan asked. "I'll show you what I've done with the files so far."

"Okay." Dena let Susan lead her to a bank of four tall metal filing cabinets. For the next four hours they sorted papers, labeled manila folders and organized them into some semblance of order. As they worked, Susan chatted about her husband and three kids, the oldest of whom was at Oklahoma State University working on a degree in veterinary medicine. The middle one was in high school and the youngest in middle school, where he was having trouble getting along with some of his classmates.

"Even a small town like Benevolence has its bad element," Susan said. "Leave it to Dean to go with them. I know at least two of the boys he hangs around with smokes. If I ever catch him with cigarettes, I'll make him eat them, package and all."

So it went until noon, when the office closed for lunch. Greg left for a meeting with some city council members. Susan took Dena around the corner for lunch at a small café with checkered tablecloths. Dena ordered a chicken sandwich, which was very good. They left the café and walked back to the office.

"I've got some grant work I need to do," Susan announced. She handed Dena several folders. "This is some history of the Main Street project, the Oklahoma towns participating, and some of the things Main Street has done. If you'll read that and grab the phone when it rings, that'd be great. We can finish those files later."

"Sounds good to me," Dena said, relieved for a chance to do something other than sort papers. She took the folders and sat at a desk, where she spent the remainder of the day reading and half-listening to Susan talk about her children.

"Greg said you're divorced."

Dena stopped reading, unsure at first she'd heard right. "Pardon me?"

"You're divorced? Greg said something about it," Susan repeated.

"Oh. Yes. Yes, I am. Just recently," Dena said.

"Was he screwing around? If you don't mind my asking," Susan said.

Dena hesitated, then lied. "No. Not that I know of."

"Oh. So what happened?"

"I'd really rather not talk about that," Dena said.

"I understand," Susan said, nodding. She then launched into a story about her oldest son's recent traumatic breakup with a girl.

Greg returned, waved and said he had to make some calls. He disappeared into his private office at the back of the building and didn't return before Susan announced that it was five o'clock and time to call it a day.

Dena grabbed her purse and hurried to the daycare. Brianna ran to greet Dena, her arms held above her head as she raced across the room calling, "Momma! Momma!"

"Don't let her fool you," Nancy said, stepping up behind Dena as she scooped Brianna into her arms. "She fussed for a while after she realized you were gone this morning, and again after her nap, but most of the time she played with the other kids and had a blast. She gets along really well with the other kids."

"That's good," Dena said, hugging Brianna. "Did you miss Mommy?" For answer, Brianna puckered up and gave her mother a kiss.

"Rebecca is in here," Nancy said, motioning to another room.

Dena found her oldest daughter sitting at a table with two other girls. One of the girls was drawing a picture while Rebecca and the other one watched. "This is what happened to them," the artist said.

"Debbie, we do not make that kind of picture here," Nancy said. She pulled the paper away from the girl and wadded it up, but not before Dena saw that it was a picture of a tree with two people hanging from a limb, ropes around their necks.

"Mommy, Debbie and Karen say the people who used to live in our house got hung," Rebecca said. "Is that true?"

"I wouldn't know," Dena answered.

"Debbie, Karen, you know better than to tell those stories," Nancy scolded the girls.

"But it's true," the blonde named Karen argued.

"My daddy said his daddy helped do it," Debbie, a redhead with a freckled face, added.

"That was a long time ago, and certainly not anything to be proud of," Nancy said. "Now, you go play. I'm going to have to tell your mothers about this." Pouting, the girls left the table.

"I'm sorry," Nancy said, turning to Dena. "They're usually not like that. But, I suppose you've heard a lot about the house you live in."

"Just a little," Dena said.

"Well, I'm sorry. I'll make sure the children don't do anything like this again."

"Thank you," Dena said. She asked Rebecca, "Are you ready to go home?"

"Can we have McDonald's for supper again?"

"No, dumpling, we're going to eat home cooking tonight?"

"Can I have spaghetti with mushrooms?"

"Yes," Dena said. "Now come on, let's go home."

Chapter 9

Dena had the girls in the front yard and was trimming the bush she'd suspected of scratching Brianna's window when the newspaper reporter came by. He introduced himself as Robert Welch and handed Dena a business card with the his name and the name of the paper, *The Benevolence Bugle*, printed on it.

"What can I do for you," Dena asked.

"Well, it's about your house," he answered. He smiled, showing small, straight teeth. He wore squared, wire-rimmed glasses and his blond hair was combed back, Jack Nicholson-style.

"What about it?"

"Well, rumor has it that it's haunted," Robert said.

"Really?"

"Yes, ma'am. You know, it hasn't been lived in for a lot of years. I heard that somebody – you – had moved in, so I thought maybe I'd come by and talk to you and see if anything strange has happened."

"I see," Dena said. "Would you like to come inside, Mr. Welch? We could sit down."

Dena saw that he cast a nervous but excited glance toward the front door before answering. "Sure. I'd love to."

Dena called her girls to her and asked Rebecca to take Brianna to the back yard to play for a while. "Keep the gate closed," she called as Rebecca led her sister away by the hand. She left her clippers on the porch and showed the reporter inside, noting how he looked the living room over thoroughly as soon as he entered. They sat on separate ends of the couch.

"You have it decorated very nice," Robert said.

"Thank you."

"Do you mind if I record our conversation?" he asked. "Just so I get my notes right?"

"No, I don't mind," Dena said. She watched him remove a small black tape recorder from his shirt pocket, push the red "Record" button and put it on the coffee table, the microphone pointed toward her, a red LCD light staring at her like an evil eye. She felt a moment of discomfort before looking away. The reporter had pulled a spiral notebook from the back pocket of his pants.

"I mostly work from written notes and use the tape for a backup," he explained. "How long have you been in the house?"

"Just a few days," Dena said. "We moved in over the weekend."

"Where are you from?"

"I grew up in Tulsa, but we moved here from Enid."

"Any connections in Benevolence? Family? Friends?"

"No. I found a job here, with the Main Street Authority, as a secretary."

"Oh, good," he said, scribbling and taking a moment to look over his notebook and smile at her. "I work with Greg quite a bit, writing about what they're doing. Is it just you and the two girls living here?"

"Yes. They're my daughters."

"Okay. Fine." He scribbled, asked their ages, scribbled some more. "Tell me, had you heard anything about this house before you moved in?"

"No. Not really. Just what the landlord said about the back part and upstairs being new. He said the people who built that got transferred by their job or something."

"Harry Bosco said that?" Robert paused in his writing.

"Yes."

"Hmm. That isn't true. The last person to live here, back in the early 1990s, was found dead in the bathtub. His name was Brian Light. He had a heart condition," Robert said slowly. "His death was ruled a heart attack, but the county medical examiner said it looked like he died of fright. Said he died screaming."

Dena sat quietly for a moment, biting her lip. "Are ... are you sure about that?"

"Yes. My editor wrote the story, back when he was still a reporter."

"I see." Dena looked toward the front door, then toward the phone. "He's the only one to die in the house?"

"Well, no, he's not. He was just the most recent."

"Most recent?" Dena locked eyes with the reporter.

"You haven't heard the history of the house since you moved in?"

"No." Dena's mouth and throat felt very dry.

"Tell me, Ms. Harris, has anything strange happened since you moved in?"

"I ... umm ... I don't think anything supernatural has happened," Dena said. "No, nothing I'd call supernatural. I haven't seen any ghosts." She tried to laugh but it sounded nervous and strained.

"Ms. Harris, forgive me, but I have to confess that I've been fascinated by this house for a long, long time," Robert said. "My grandfather was a reporter, too, and he covered the events that happened here back in the 1920s.

Since then, only one family, not counting Brian Light, who was a bachelor, has lived here. That family told several people about some bizarre things happening before they left town. They didn't pack or anything. They had a barbecue with their neighbors one evening, and later that same night the neighbors heard screaming, looked out their windows and saw the Painter family jumping into their car. They drove away and were never seen around here again."

"What happened here in the 1920s?" Dena asked.

"Well, the short of it is that Matthew Astor was murdered by his wife and son," Robert said. "Then, the townspeople formed a lynch mob and hung them from a tree in that park behind your house."

"That's the short version? There's more detail?" Dena asked reluctantly.

"Well, yeah ..." Robert trailed off, his eyes moving to the tape recorder. "That's strange. Those were brand new batteries." Just before he picked up the device, Dena saw that the red LCD light had faded to a bare glow. "Excuse me just a second while I replace these." He quickly popped out the old batteries and replaced them with new ones from another pants pocket. He turned the machine on and replaced it on the table.

"What is the rest of the story?" Dena asked.

"Well, it's all pretty strange. Strange and sick," Robert said. "You see, Matthew Astor's wife, Rosalyn, was also his sister. Of course, nobody knew that until after they were all dead. My grandfather found that piece of information by researching records in St. Louis, where they lived before coming to Indian Territory.

"By that time, it wasn't so surprising because

everybody knew Rosalyn and Matt Jr., the son, were also lovers and had killed the old man for the fortune he'd made from bootlegging."

"You mean ..."

"That's right," Robert nodded. "Incest between brother and sister, then mother and son. And murder. Neighbors of the Astors in St. Louis also said old Rosalyn was a witch, that she sacrificed cats in the backyard and wrote messages in their blood. One neighbor claimed to have seen Rosalyn chanting a spell as she drained the blood of a rabbit over the older Matt's ... well, over his penis."

"What did they – the Painter family – say was happening here?" Dena asked.

"Noises, mostly," the reporter answered. "Arguing, whispers, banging noises, that kind of thing. Doors wouldn't stay closed. Lanterns and candles were blown out. They'd planned to have the house wired for electricity but left before it happened. Oh, and digging. The father, Max Painter, swore he heard the sounds of digging.

"By the way, the body of old Matthew Astor was never found. His son confessed that he and Rosalyn killed the old man, but he wouldn't say what they did with the body. He had the rope around his neck already when he confessed. Eyewitness accounts say Rosalyn started mumbling something, then Matt Jr. started choking like he was swallowing his tongue. He wouldn't, or couldn't, say any more, so the mob hung them both."

"That's – that's all very ... sad," Dena said. "You certainly do know a lot about this house. What about the other man, the one who died in the bathtub? Did he ... did he have any problems?"

"Other than being scared to death?" Robert gave a short laugh, then stopped. "Sorry. No, ma'am, he didn't make any complaints. He hadn't been in the house very long. He was divorced, in his fifties and engaged to a single mother with three kids. He bought this house pretty cheap and built all the additions your landlord told you about. Then he moved in and was living here while waiting for his fiancé to arrive from, I think it was Chicago. He died before she ever saw the house."

Dena sat quietly, thinking. She slowly realized the house had grown dark and looked toward a window. The evening was getting late. "Excuse me, I have to get my daughters in. I can't believe they haven't already come in on their own."

She went to the back door and found Rebecca and Brianna squatted over something in the back yard. Rebecca was pointing at the ground. Brianna squealed, laughed and pointed at the same thing. It was too dark for Dena to see what it was they were looking at. She opened the door and went into the yard.

"What are you girls doing?"

"Momma!" Brianna ran toward her, her arms held above her head, a smile on her face. She grabbed Dena by the shorts and shouted, "Go!" She began pulling Dena back to where Rebecca waited.

"It's a frog," Rebecca said. "A really big one."

Dena looked where her daughters were pointing and saw the biggest bullfrog she'd ever seen, it's skin appearing to be almost black in the fading light.

"I poked it and it won't hop," Rebecca said. "It just grunts."

"Leave it alone," Dena said. "How would you like it if

someone was poking you?"

Suddenly the frog launched itself from the ground, hit Dena in the left thigh and fell back to the grass. All three females screamed. Dena jumped back, her hands going to her leg, rubbing at the place where she'd been hit. It didn't hurt, but she didn't like the feeling. The frog squatted motionless, ignoring them.

"Come on, girls," Dena said. "It's past time to come in. Rebecca, I need you to take a bath with your sister. I need to finish talking to the reporter."

"What's he want?"

"Oh, he's writing a newspaper story about the house," Dena said.

"Did you tell him about my closet door? And about the lights burning out?"

"No, Rebecca, I didn't. And I don't want you to say anything, either. Understand?"

"Why not?"

"Because I said." Dena stopped, her hand on the door handle, her eyes fixed on her oldest child. "Understand?"

"Okay."

"All right. Go get your pajamas. And some clean underwear. You can bathe downstairs. I don't want Brianna upstairs while I can't be there." Dena scooped the toddler up in her arms and went back to the living room.

Robert Welch was snoring on her couch. Keeping her eyes on him, Dena reached over and turned on a lamp. The reporter continued snoring without noticing the light. Dena carried Brianna into the bathroom and started running water into the tub. She had Brianna stripped down to her diaper when Rebecca arrived.

"Mom, he's asleep. Is he going to sleep here all night?"

Rebecca asked.

"Of course not," Dena answered. "He must have just been tired. You get Brianna in the tub. You both need your hair washed, too. I'll go wake him up." Dena turned to leave, then paused, her eyes lingering on the bathtub. *Is that where Brian Light died?*

"She didn't harvest any booty fruit in her diaper, did she?" Rebecca asked.

"Huh?" Dena shook her gaze from the tub.

"Does she have any booty fruit in her diaper?" Rebecca repeated.

"No. And don't call it that," Dena said. "She's just wet. No poop."

"That's what Daddy calls it."

"I know," Dena said, her voice stern. She left the bathroom, closing the door behind her, and went to the couch.

"Mr. Welch," she said. No response. "Mr. Welch?" The man continued snoring. Dena noted that the red eye on his tape recorder was dead again, though the "Record" button was still down. Dena reached out and nudged the man's shoulder and repeated his name. He shifted, farted, and continued snoring. She nudged him again, harder.

"Huh? What?" The reporter raised his head and opened bleary eyes. He squinted at Dena for a moment, then jerked to full attention. "My God, I am so sorry," he said. "Was I asleep?"

"Very much asleep," Dena said, smiling. "Been working too hard?"

"I ... uhh ... Listen, I'm really sorry about that," he said, blushing. "I should go. We can finish this some other time. If you don't mind?" He stood up and fidgeted with his notebook and pen.

"Really, Mr. Welch, I'm afraid I don't have anything to add to the story," Dena said. "Nothing's happened."

"Oh. Uh-huh. Well, okay then. Thank you for your time," he said, backing toward the door. Dena stepped toward him to see him out. He paused and looked at her earnestly for a moment. "Was there anybody else in here when you came back?"

"Just you. Why?"

"I ... thought I heard someone."

"You were snoring pretty loud," Dena said.

"Oh. Uh-huh. Thank you again, Ms. Harris." He turned and practically ran out the door. The screen door slammed shut. Dena walked over to close the main door; she heard the reporter's car come to life and the tires squealing as he pulled away. She closed the door and started toward the bathroom.

In his haste, Robert Welch had left his little tape recorder on the table. Dena picked it up and hit the "Stop" button. She put the machine on her mantle and went to the bathroom, where Rebecca was lifting Brianna out of the tub. She helped the girls get dried off, combed out their hair, had the nightly argument with Rebecca over sleeping in her own bed, sent her upstairs and got Brianna tucked into her crib.

Dena sat on the couch and stared at the nightly news without absorbing any of it. Her thoughts remained on the story the reporter had told her. She looked toward the mantle, got up and grabbed the tape recorder. She sat down at the kitchen table and plugged two new AA batteries into the recorder. She rewound the tape and hit "Play."

Dena had always hated the Okie twang of her own voice on tape. She listened patiently to the last few minutes of her conversation with Robert Welch. She excused herself to go get the girls. Silence followed for a couple of seconds, then some tapping that could have been the reporter hitting his notepad with his pen. The tapping stopped. Silence.

"Get out. If you value your life, get out." The male voice was faint, as if yelled from a great distance. The warning had hardly ended before the reporter's snoring could be heard on the tape; he was snoring lightly, nowhere near as deeply asleep as he'd been when Dena found him.

A new voice, a female voice, shrieked, "Get away from him!"

"Witch!" the first voice, the man's, yelled. The single word was distorted, as if the batteries in the recorder had suddenly lost a huge amount of their power.

"Get away," the female screamed.

A new male voice entered the conversation. "Mom, don't – "

The first male voice returned, apparently addressing the reporter again. "She'll kill you like she killed ..."

The voice faded to distortion. Then silence.

Dena turned off the machine and left it on the table.

Steven E. Wedel

DAY FIVE

Chapter 10

Dena awoke feeling as if she'd gotten no rest. The sleepiness hung on her like a drunkenness, making her groggy and dull. She rolled over in the bed and found herself face-to-face with Brianna. Rebecca lay on the other side of the baby. Both girls were sound asleep.

Dena stared at them, wondering when they'd come to her bed, when she'd taken Brianna from her crib. She had no recollection of leaving her bed. She knew she'd been tired. She even had skipped her nightly shower, going to bed right after listening to the reporter's tape recording.

With a great surge of effort, Dena pushed the covers off herself and sat up. She slumped forward, not wanting to get to her feet, but finally drove herself to do it. She stumbled into the bathroom and stripped off the T-shirt and panties she wore to bed, sat on the toilet to relieve herself and started the bathtub faucet at the same time.

The cold water of the shower helped wake her up, but she couldn't take much of it before adjusting the faucet to get warmer water. She showered slowly, washing herself and shaving her armpits. She checked her legs and decided they could wait until that evening. She turned off the water, but hesitated a moment before opening the shower door, remembering what she thought she'd seen last time. Finally, she slid the door open. Despite the exhaust fan, the room still had a thin fog of steam swirling around it. But no shapes in the steam. Dena stepped from the shower and reached for a towel. That's when she saw the writing in the condensation on the medicine cabinet mirror.

BABY

DANGER

Dena burst through the bathroom doorway and rounded the corner to her bedroom. Both Brianna and Rebecca were still fast asleep. She looked around the room. Nothing was disturbed. There was no one hiding in the corners. Slowly, her eyes staying on the bed where her daughters slept, Dena retreated to the bathroom doorway. She darted inside, grabbed her towel and her nightshirt, and returned to the hallway. She dried herself and pulled the shirt over her head, keeping her eyes on her bedroom.

Finally, she looked back at the mirror, hoping she'd been mistaken and there really wasn't any writing.

Streaks of condensation had run down the glass, leaving shiny lines like varicose veins on the surface of the wet mirror. Any words that had been written on the glass were distorted beyond recognition.

It was nothing. Just streaks and my tired mind playing tricks on me.

Dena backed up and looked into Brianna's room. She couldn't find anything out of the ordinary. She went through the first floor of the house, looking for evidence of an intruder. She went upstairs. Nothing. She was downstairs, walking through the dining area to the kitchen when she saw the basement door. It was slightly ajar. There was a pantry just inside the door and Dena knew Rebecca had opened the door yesterday to get a can of green beans for dinner. She hadn't noticed the door still being open after that, but she couldn't remember looking.

Reluctantly, Dena opened door. The smell of damp

underground was claustrophobic. She flicked a switch and the narrow wooden stairwell was illuminated. She took a flashlight from a shelf beside the canned goods and turned it on. Fortunately, it worked, though the beam was dim. Barefoot, wearing nothing but the T-shirt that hung just past her crotch, Dena started town the creaking stairs.

She'd only been in the basement of the house once. She hadn't liked it. Three of the walls and floor were nothing but packed dirt. Some old wooden shelves lined one wall and another was covered with wood and had a door that opened onto the hot water tank and central heat unit. The only light in the basement was in the enclosed area for the water tank and heating unit.

Dena rounded the turn in the stairs and waved her light through the dim basement. She didn't see any unusual shapes, no movement. She stepped onto the cold dirt floor and walked to the door of the area housing the appliances. She opened it, looked quickly inside, then closed it and stepped back. She stepped onto a small pile of loose dirt.

Dena trained her light on the floor. The pile of loose dirt was small, only an inch or so deep and maybe six inches in diameter. She trailed the light up the wall and found some cracks in the packed earth.

Settling? The dry weather? Rats?

Even the thought of invading rodents would have been welcome in the current circumstances. As it was, she had no explanation.

Then her light faded and died.

Dena moved quickly toward the stairs and hurried up them into the well-lit dining area. She closed the basement door, pressing it into the frame for a moment before letting it go. She went back to the bathroom. The mirror was clear.

Dena went to wake her daughters. It was not an easy task, as they both seemed to be as reluctant to wake up as Dena had been. Finally, she had them roused, dressed and fed. They piled into the little car and Dena dropped them off at their appropriate destinations, then went for her second day on the new job.

Squatting around the lowest drawer in one of the file cabinets, Dena was alphabetizing records and nodding every once in a while as Susan recounted some story about her son when Robert Welch entered the office. He was wearing jeans, a maroon polo shirt and a tan sports coat.

"Hi Robert," Susan bleated when the bell over the door sounded. She got to her feet and went to meet the reporter. "Did you get that press release about the old Olson's store? I really think we'll get a grant to help renovate that for a teen center."

"Yes, I got it. Thanks," the reporter said. "I came by to see Ms. Harris. Will that be all right? You don't have her too busy, do you?"

"She'd probably enjoy the break from listening to me," Susan said, laughing. She held a hand to her mouth as if blocking the sound from traveling in Dena's direction and whispered loudly, "She's single, you know."

Dena saw the reporter give Susan a barely hidden look of irritation as he moved around her and approached the bank of file cabinets. Susan took a seat at the computer terminal and called up her personal Yahoo e-mail account. Dena got to her feet and shook Robert's outstretched hand.

"Nice to see you again," she said.

"Same here." He nodded and looked very sheepish.

"Again, I'm really sorry about last night. I don't know what came over me. I – "

"Last night?" Susan interrupted. "Sounds like you two have already gotten acquainted. You always were a sly dog, Robert."

"Do you get a morning break," Robert asked Dena.

"I don't know," Dena said.

"Let me take you to the café for a cup of coffee. I happen to know Greg is away this morning and I'm sure Susan won't miss us for a few minutes."

"You two go ahead," Susan said. "I'll get Dena here to give me all the details when you come back."

His back to Susan, Robert rolled his eyes so Dena could see it. She covered her mouth to hide a smile and followed him out of the office and around the corner to the café.

"Like I said, I'm sorry about falling asleep on your couch," Robert said. "It was very strange. I felt myself going, but it was like sinking in quicksand. I couldn't do a damn thing about it. And then I had this dream ..."

"What kind of dream?" Dena couldn't look at him as she asked.

"People arguing," Robert said. "It was so bizarre. One of them wanted to kill me and two others were arguing with her. I remember ... well, it was only a dream."

"Tell me," Dena urged. "What do you remember?"

"The one who wanted to kill me. She ... she touched me. But it was like she touched inside me. I don't know. It's all strange. I was probably just worked up about finally being in that house."

"You'd never been inside before?"

"Nope."

Dena was silent for a moment, not sure what to say. Finally, she said, "Well, you didn't have to go to the trouble of stopping by to apologize for falling asleep. I'm sorry I was so boring."

They both laughed, then Robert said, "Yeah, well, I also came by to ask if I left my tape recorder on your coffee table. I think I did."

"Yes, you did," Dena said.

"Any chance you have it with you?"

"No. I left it at home. I meant to bring it. I was going to bring it over to your office, but ..." She paused, not sure how to finish. "This morning was just kind of crazy. You know how kids are."

"Not really. I don't have any and don't remember anything I could possibly have done to make my parents think I was anything but pure joy."

"Oh, I bet," Dena laughed. "I can bring the recorder tomorrow, or you can come by and get it. Or, I could run home at lunch."

"No need for that. I have a city council meeting tonight, but I have a spare recorder I can take. How about if I just come by and get it Friday evening?"

"Okay."

"And, can I take you to dinner when I pick it up?" His face flushed scarlet as he asked.

Dena sputtered for a moment, then raised her cup and took a drink of coffee. She put it down, stirred the liquid slowly. "I don't know. I'm not sure that's a good idea. I haven't been on a date in a long time. I just got divorced. I don't know if I'm ready. You know?"

"How about if we don't think of it as a date?" Robert asked. "You're new to town. How about if I take you and your girls out for dinner, then show you the sights?"

Dena laughed nervously. "Actually, the girls will be away this weekend. Their dad will be here to take them back to Enid Friday evening."

"Then it's just you and me?"

"I guess."

"So, you're saying you'll go?"

Dena nodded, then smiled. "Susan was right. You are a sly dog."

"Susan talks waaaaaaay too much," Robert said.

"I should get back over there," Dena said.

"Dena, are you sure nothing strange has happened to you in that house?"

Lying to him suddenly had a new depth, Dena realized. Still, she couldn't bring herself to say anything about the events. "Nothing that can't be explained logically," she said.

"Like what?"

"Oh, nothing. Really." She couldn't meet his eyes. *He'll hear the voices on his tape.* Dena wondered if she should erase that part of the tape. *Would that be so bad?* "How about if we talk about this on Friday?"

"Then there is something?"

"Maybe. I don't know. I just don't know."

"Be careful, Dena. I don't want to sound ... well, like I'm probably sounding right now ... like a superstitious freak, but I really believe there's something strange about that house. I thought it before I came over and I think it even more now. My card that I gave you has my cell phone number on it. Please call me if you need anything. Okay? Anything at all."

"Okay. And, thanks. I do appreciate the concern.

Unless you're just being so nice in hopes of getting a *National Enquirer* story."

"Oh, puh-leeze!" Robert said in mock agony. "I wouldn't dream of using you for a story. You've never slept with the president, have you?"

"Not lately, no," Dena said. "Really, I have to get back. It's only my second day and I've run out like this."

"Don't worry about it. Greg is an easy-going guy. Get your work done and he won't have a problem with you slipping out for a while."

Robert walked her back to the office and left her outside the door, saying he didn't want to have to visit with Susan any more that day. Dena wished she could do the same, as Susan began firing questions at her as soon as the entered the office.

Dena got out of eating lunch with Susan by saying she had some personal errands to run. As soon as she had the office to herself, she called her landlord. Harry Bosco picked up on the fourth ring.

"Mr. Bosco, this is Dena Harris. I just rented the house on South Twelfth."

"Yes, Dena. What can I do for you?"

"Well, I was just wondering if you'd kept a key to the house for yourself?"

"Yes."

"You, umm ... I'm sorry to ask this, but ... you weren't in the house this morning, were you?"

"No."

"Does anybody else have a key?"

"Not unless you've given them one."

"Mr. Bosco, why didn't you tell me about the people who died in there?"

"What? Who told you people died in there?"

"Please, Mr. Bosco, the house seems to be some kind of legend here in town. The Astors and that other guy, the one who added on to the house. Why didn't you tell me that?"

"That's just nonsense. You're a big girl. Surely you don't believe in ghost stories?" He tried to laugh it off, but that only irritated Dena more.

"Mr. Bosco, you didn't represent the house fairly to me," she said. "I want out of my lease."

"Now, hold on," he said, his voice suddenly serious again. "You signed a one-year lease. I'm sorry, but I have to hold you to that."

"We could go to court."

"Come on, Ms. Harris, be reasonable. Are you going to tell a judge you want out because you're scared of Matthew Astor's ghost?"

Dena couldn't think of a response. The landlord had a point. Plus, there really weren't any other houses to choose from. And there was no way she'd get her deposit back, and she knew she'd need that money to pay for another place.

"All right, Mr. Bosco. Fine. However, there are some cracks in the wall in the basement. Your responsibility in the lease is to fix that kind of thing. I expect you to do it."

"Oh, that'll happen with those dirt basements," he said, his voice once again a friendly drawl. "What you want to do is just turn on the hose and run some water along the foundation. They'll crack just because the ground's gotten so dry this year."

"Fine. Thank you." Dena hung up the phone.

The rest of the afternoon was uneventful. When five

o'clock finally rolled around, Dena was relieved to get out of the office and away from Susan's endless prattle, but felt some trepidation about returning home. She tried to convince herself that was silly, but the urge to stay away was strong enough that she easily gave in to Rebecca's request to go to McDonald's for dinner.

Chapter 11

The phone was ringing when the family returned home. Dena hurried to pick it up. As she put the receiver to her ear, every light in the downstairs part of the house came to life, rose to blinding intensity, then shattered into isolated rain showers of tiny glass fragments. Dena screamed and dropped the phone.

"Don't move!" she shouted at her daughters. She crunched over glass on the living room floor until she got to the girls. She carried them, one by one, to the dining room, where she put them in chairs and commanded that they not move. She took the electric vacuum cleaner and went back to the living room. Just before she flicked the switch to start the machine, she heard someone calling her name.

Slowly, Dena looked around the room, the blood draining from her face, her hands beginning to tremble on the handle of the sweeper. Then she saw the receiver of the phone laying on the floor. She picked it up and put it carefully to her ear.

"Hello," she said timidly.

"Dena? What the hell is going on there?" Danny asked.

"Nothing," Dena said. "The lights just came on and burned out."

"That's nothing? How many of them did that?"

"I don't know. All of them downstairs, at least. We go through a lot of light bulbs here. The landlord says there's no wiring problem. Idiot. What do you want?"

"Sounds like you're having a bad day."

"Come on, Danny, what do you want?" Dena demanded of her ex-husband.

"I want to talk to my family," he said.

"Uh-huh."

"Listen, how about if I come over tomorrow after work? I could bring over those lawn chairs you said you want."

"You can bring them on Friday when you come for the girls."

"Dena, give me a break," he began to whine. "I want to see you. I'll sleep on the couch and not be a bother. Maybe I can poke around on Friday and see if I can find your wiring problem, then when Rebecca gets out of school, I'll bring the girls home for the weekend. It'll save you having to meet me halfway between Benevolence and Enid."

"Listen to me, Danny," Dena said, her eyes fixed on a window where the evening light was quickly dying. "We are divorced. It's over. You can't give me what I want and I'm not what you want."

"I *do* want you."

"I don't have a dick, Danny!" Dena screamed. "I never had one and I never will. I can't stand to have you touch me while you're thinking about some guy in your platoon. I can't do it." Dena sagged against the wall, crying.

"Dena …"

"No. Don't do this to me, Danny. Isn't it enough that you admitted you never loved me? That you married me just to have kids? I haven't told anyone what you are because you say you'd lose your job. Doesn't that count for anything? Even my own mother doesn't know why I left you. You … you prick. Why can't you leave us alone?"

"Dena? Are you okay? I – "

He was interrupted by the television and stereo; both appliances came on of their own accord, the volume on each rising in a rapid crescendo until they were deafening. Dena screamed again and dropped the phone. She ran to the entertainment center and hit the power button on each. The silence was sudden and deafening.

"Dena? Dena?" Danny's voice called from the phone. Reluctantly, Dena picked up the receiver again. In the dining room, she could hear both her girls crying.

"Fine," Dena said into the phone. "You can come tomorrow. You try anything with me – I mean so much as a good-night kiss – and I swear to God I'll tell your commanding officer about what you and that private did last summer."

"Dena, you – "

"Do I make myself clear, Daniel Wahl?"

"Yes, Dena. Dena?"

"What?"

"Thank you."

"Good bye." Dena hung up the phone.

"Mommeeeeeeeeeeeeeee?"

"I'm coming," Dena called. She went to the dining room. Both girls started to get up, but Dena waved them back into their chairs. "Stay there. I have to sweep up the glass." She hugged them both, wiped their tears and kissed their foreheads. Then she went back to the living room and turned on the vacuum cleaner.

The glass was so fine that much of what she cleaned

was little more than powder. Dena went over all the living room carpet until there was no more rattling noise to indicate the sweeper was picking up anything. She started for the kitchen so she could do the carpet in the dining room.

At the threshold of the kitchen, she encountered resistance. Some unseen force was pushing back on the vacuum cleaner as if trying to keep Dena in the living room. She looked into the dining room and saw that both her daughters had their heads on the table and were fast asleep.

"Rebecca! Brianna!" Dena shouted. She turned off the sweeper and called again. Still, neither girl stirred. Dena shoved the sweeper forward. Just as violently, it was pushed back at her.

"Stop it, Mother," a voice said. Dena recognized it as one of the voices she'd heard on Robert's tape recorder. A woman's laughter, high and maniacal, filled the darkening house. The male voice spoke again, saying, "Leave them alone. Leave them alone, Mother!"

Suddenly, the force holding Dena back was pulled away. She jumped forward, toward her daughters, but after a couple of steps she was smacked as if by a huge invisible hand. She flew back through the doorway and sprawled on the living room floor, her flesh stinging from her knees to her scalp. Ignoring the pain, she rolled to her feet and ran back into the kitchen, expecting at any moment to encounter the invisible force again. There was nothing.

Dena grabbed both her girls and shook them until they woke up. Both of them started crying, reaching for her and clinging to her neck. Dena remained hunched over the table with her daughters hanging from her, all of them crying, for several moments. Finally, she got herself under control and slowly calmed her girls.

"I fell asleep and had a bad dream," Rebecca said.

"Shush, it's all right now," Dena said. "It was just a dream."

"Somebody wanted to take Bree away from us," Rebecca said. "Somebody really mean."

"Nobody's going to take my girls away from me," Dena said. "It was just a dream."

"She said if I tried to stop her, she'd kill me and my … and my … " Rebecca's voiced hitched and her bottom lip began to quiver as fresh tears rose to her eyes. "And my mommy," she said as the tears spilled down her cheeks.

"Hush, baby, hush," Dena said. "Nobody's going to do any of those things."

"I don't want to stay here tonight," Rebecca said. Brianna, seeing her sister crying again, also resumed bawling.

"Come on, girls, please," Dena pleaded. "Stop. I need to finish sweeping. Let me get this glass up so we can at least walk around. Okay?" Rebecca nodded, but Brianna only held out her pudgy arms, wanting to be picked up. Dena sighed and lifted the toddler from her chair. Carrying her baby, Dena swept the dining room floor, then did hers and Brianna's bedrooms and the downstairs bathroom with Rebecca staying close behind her.

"Okay, that's all of it," Dena said, shutting off the machine. "Still, we should be careful where we step for a while, just in case I missed anything."

"Are you going to put new light bobs in, Mommy?" Rebecca asked.

"Bulbs, sweetie. Light bulbs," Dena said absently.

There's only one left. I'm down to a few dollars in my wallet to last until my first paycheck. Shit! "No, baby, I'm not. We'll be like the pioneers again tonight and use candles."

"I don't wanna ..."

"I don't, either, dumpling, but we don't have much of a choice," Dena snapped. "I'll call the landlord again tomorrow and make him get out here and look at the wiring to see why this keeps happening. Until then, I'm not putting in any more light bobs. Bulbs!

"Now, you two should take a bath before it gets any darker," Dena said, going into the bathroom and turning on the faucet at the tub. "You can take one together again."

"But Mommy, what about the water? I don't want to stay here."

Dena started to answer harshly but held her tongue. The memory of the invisible force holding the vacuum cleaner back was still too fresh. Her face still stung where the unseen, giant hand had slapped her. She didn't want to stay in the house, either. But the only alternative was sleeping in the car. There wasn't enough money for a motel room. *Maybe I imagined it all. Maybe the vacuum was stuck on something.* She didn't completely buy it, but clung to it nonetheless.

"We've got nowhere else to go, dumpling. We're staying here. We'll be all right. Now, let's get you two into the bathtub."

"What about the water?" Rebecca whined.

"What about it?"

"You know. What if it starts moving by itself again?"

"Honey, that was some kind of bug in the water."

"No it wasn't."

Dena knew she'd never make an argument sound believable. "You still have to take a bath," she said. "I'll stay in here with you. We'll just wash and get out. Then you can go to sleep in my bed. We'll all sleep in my bed tonight."

Dena got the girls bathed and dressed for bed. She tucked them into her bed, Rebecca on one side and Brianna in the middle. She expected to have some trouble with the toddler, but Brianna was tired enough that she stuck her pacifier in her mouth and settled right down. Dena slipped out of the room, leaving the door open behind her.

She gathered a collection of candles and returned to the bathroom, where she lit a half-dozen, placing them on the toilet tank and around the sink. She closed the door most of the way, leaving it open only a crack, hoping she'd be able to hear her girls if there was any problem. Then, she ran fresh water into the tub, stripped off her clothes and settled into the bath. Dena washed quickly, then lathered her legs with shaving cream and reached for her razor.

"Blooooooooood …"

Dena suddenly felt cold and more naked than her lack of clothing could account for. The plastic handle of her razor snapped before she realized she was pressing the blade against her leg. The realization brought the pain of the cut she'd made just above her right ankle. Instinctively, she dropped the leg under the water. The shaving cream sloughed off, creating a white scum on the surface of the water … a white scum tinged with pink where the blood was rising from the cut on her ankle. Dena raised the leg again to look at the cut.

Blood mixed with water and streamed off her leg. Despite the rivulets of crimson, Dena determined the cut wasn't so bad. She lowered her leg into the water again, where the blood rose from her flesh to the surface of the water ... and beyond.

Her eyes wide with disbelief, Dena watched the tendrils of blood rise from the water, spreading like mist, until the very vague form of a man was kneeling beside the tub. She opened her mouth and tried to scream, but her throat was too dry, her tongue swollen like a dead thing in her mouth.

"Don't be afraid of me," the shape said. It was the same voice that had whispered about blood a moment before Dena cut herself. Dena shrank away from the thing, toward the back of the bathtub. "Don't be afraid," the shape repeated. "There is power in the blood. She knows that and will try to use it to be reborn. For now, she is distracted, but that never lasts long."

Her jaw quivering, Dena asked, "Who are you?"

"My name is Brian Light. The reporter told you about me."

Dena heard herself moaning. She stared at the thing beside the tub, something so transparent she couldn't be sure it was real – except for the pink tinge of her own blood hanging in the air like the thinnest wisp of smoke. Her leg had nearly stopped bleeding. The shape beside the tub became less and less distinct.

"What do you want?" Dena asked.

"I want you to leave," the voice said. "For your own good. She wants your daughter. She wants ... the baby. She ..." The smoky form began to break apart, the voice trailing away to barely a whisper. "... power in the blood

… Reborn …"

"No! Come back," Dena shouted. She raised her leg from the water and squeezed the flesh around the wound, trying to coax more blood from the cut, but only a few drops oozed out. She snatched the head of the razor from the water, but stopped before purposefully making another cut. She sat back in the tub.

"I'm losing my mind," she whispered.

Chapter 12

Dena woke up freezing and facing the closet door. She reached for a blanket at the foot of the bed and realized she had kicked it off. As she sat up, she became aware of the dark shape crouching over Brianna in the middle of the bed. She screamed and lunged toward her daughter. The air of the room suddenly seemed to shimmer as the thing on the bed shrieked. It lashed out with a shadowy arm and slapped Dena off the bed.

Dena fell to the floor, stunned, her head aching as if her brain were frozen. She shook her head, shaking away some of the feeling, and got to her feet. Rebecca was screaming and crying now. Brianna was still asleep. The black shape was howling and flailing about as if fighting invisible attackers.

"Get away from my daughter!" Dena yelled. She dove at Brianna and scooped the girl from under the shape. She hugged her youngest daughter to her and yelled at Rebecca, "Get off the bed!"

Rebecca slid off the edge and ran around the bed. Dena met her at the end of the bed and pushed her toward the door. They ran into the hallway, the black thing behind them still clawing at unseen attackers and howling like a devil. Dena slammed the door behind her.

"Mommy, what was that? What was it doing in our bed?" Rebecca cried.

"I don't know, baby. I don't know," Dena said. She held Brianna away so she could look at the girl's face. The toddler was still asleep, her lips blue. Dena touched her face and found that she was as cold as if she'd been buried in snow.

"Oh, my baby, my baby," Dena sobbed. She hurried to a linen closet and got all the spare blankets. She put Brianna on the couch, and, fumbling in the dark living room, she wrapped the girl in the blankets while Rebecca sat close by, still crying. Dena rubbed Brianna's face, then her blanketed arms and legs, then her face again. Slowly, some color returned to the girl's cheeks and lips. Then her eyelids fluttered and opened.

"Momma," she said and tried to reach for Dena, her arms held to her side by the wrapped blankets.

Fresh tears burst from Dena's eyes and she fell over the girl, hugging her close, her arms getting under the blankets to squeeze the girl tighter. She lay over Brianna, crying for a while, then sat up, pulling the girl up with her and holding her against her breast. Rebecca scooted closer to her and Dena put an arm around her.

The house was silent. No howling from the bedroom. No passing cars. No ticking clocks. Dead silence.

"Mommy, what are we going to do?" Rebecca asked.

Dena couldn't answer for a while. Finally, she had an idea. "I want you and Bree to stay right here on the couch," she said. "But I want you to keep talking to me so I know you're okay. I'm going back to my room to get some clothes, then I'm going to Bree's room and yours. We're going to a motel for the night."

"What should I say?" Rebecca asked.

"I don't know. Anything. Just keep saying 'We're okay.' Can you do that?"

Rebecca nodded, so Dena got up, put Brianna down

carefully next to her sister. She could see the toddler's eyes in the dimness of the room. Brianna was awake, but her face had a haunted look, as if she'd seen the very fires of hell and had returned shell-shocked. "I'll be right back, sweetie," she said, bending to kiss first Brianna, then Rebecca. She turned and started for her bedroom.

"We're okay. We're okay. We're okay," Rebecca said behind her.

Dena turned the knob and pushed open her bedroom door. The room was dark, darker than the living room, with only a tiny bit of moonlight coming in around the Venetian blind over the window. Dena tried the light switch, knowing the bulb was burned out. Nothing. The bed appeared empty. Dena moved in quickly, going to the closet and grabbing her old gym bag. She stuffed a pair of slacks and a blouse into the bag, slipped her feet into some shoes and plucked her purse from the dresser as she left the room.

"Aaaaaannnnnieeeeee ..." A voice whispered behind her, then the house filled with manic laughter.

"Mommy!" Rebecca shouted. Dena had been going up the hallway to Brianna's room. She dropped the bag and ran back to the living room. The girls were still on the couch, Rebecca with her hands clenched under her chin. Brianna's wide, scared eyes roved around the room sleepily.

"What?" Dena asked.

"I heard laughing. I'm scared," Rebecca said.

"Me too," Dena answered. "Just keep talking to me."

"We're okay. We're okay," Rebecca said, but her voice had no conviction.

Dena went back to the hallway, found the gym bag,

and went to the door of Brianna's room. She pushed the door open in time to see the drawers of Brianna's dresser fly out. Clothes hurtled across the room, slamming into Dena like blind birds.

"Stop it! Stop it, stop it, stop it!" Dena screamed. She grabbed some of the clothes that were hanging from her shoulders and went back to the living room.

"What happened, Mommy?"

"Nothing." Dena stuffed the clothes into the bag. The thought of going upstairs to Rebecca's room scared her. She didn't want to leave the girls so far behind, and she didn't dare carry Brianna up and down the stairs. She knew she couldn't send Rebecca up there alone.

"Deeeeeeeennnnnaaa ..." A rush of wind passed through the room, moving toward the back of the house, carrying her name with it. Rebecca screamed. Brianna began crying.

"I want my daddy," Rebecca cried.

"Let's go," Dena said. She scooped Brianna from the couch, grabbed her gym bag and purse and shepherded Rebecca toward the front door.

"What about my clothes?" Rebecca asked on the front porch. "I can't go to school in my pajamas."

"We'll think of something," Dena answered. "Go get in the car."

Dena had to unwrap Brianna to strap her into the car seat. The girl finally felt warm. She had stopped crying. Her eyelids were heavy and Dena knew she probably would be asleep before they got out of the driveway. She went back to the front porch, reached around the front door and turned the lock on the doorknob. She pulled the door closed, giving the knob a habitual twist to be sure it had locked. Dena returned to the car, got her keys from her purse, and they drove away.

"What about my clothes?" Rebecca asked again from the back seat.

"I tell you what," Dena said. "We'll go to Wal-Mart right now. I'll lock the doors and you can stay in the car with Bree. I'll run right in and buy you a new outfit for school tomorrow and run right back out. Okay?"

"I thought you said we didn't have any more money until payday."

"Well honey, we don't. I'm going to write a check and ask your father to loan me the money when he gets here tomorrow."

"Daddy's coming?"

"Yes, dear, he's coming. You get to stay with him this weekend. Remember?" For the first time, Dena realized she would be all alone in the house over the weekend.

They drove to the Wal-Mart store. Dena was very reluctant to leave her daughters alone in the car. She made Rebecca move to the front seat and gave her explicit instructions about not opening the doors or windows for anybody. "Start honking the horn if anybody tries to bother you. Okay?"

Rebecca nodded solemnly. "Are you going inside in just your pajamas?" she asked.

"Yes, dumpling, I am. Nobody will mind. I have shorts on underneath." She raised the end of her long T-shirt to show her daughter the shorts.

"Hurry, Mommy. Okay?"

"I will. I'll be right back."

Dena snatched her purse and hurried toward the front of the store, casting a final look back at the car before going inside. She grabbed a pair of jeans and a shirt with the Power Puff Girls on it, then a cheap pair of shoes and a package of socks. As an afterthought, she hurried to the pharmacy section and picked up a couple of toothbrushes, toothpaste and a can of deodorant. She felt guilty writing the check, especially including the extra cash to pay for a motel room, knowing she didn't have the money to cover it, but she took the blue plastic bag and the extra money and returned to the car, where Rebecca reported there'd been no trouble while she was gone.

"I saw a man drinking from a paper sack," the girl said.

"You did?"

"Yep. He was over by the corner of the building. He walked funny."

Dena laughed, started the car and they drove away. The cheap motel room they rented smelled stale, the carpet and ceiling were stained and the beds were lumpy. But, there were no disembodied voices, no flying clothing, no unnatural shapes and the electric lights worked. Dena put Brianna in bed with Rebecca, set the room's alarm clock and crawled under the think covers of her own bed. Within minutes, all three were sound asleep.

DAY SIX

Chapter 13

Dena couldn't focus on even the most mundane aspects of her job that morning. She found herself misfiling folders, making countless typos at the keyboard, and at one point she knocked over Susan's coffee mug, sending the woman's concoction of coffee and sugar spilling across the desk and some grant paperwork.

Dena stared at the mess for a moment, then broke down crying.

"Oh, honey, what is it?" Susan said, the harsh look falling from her face as she put her hands on Dena's shoulders. "What is it? I bet it's man-trouble, isn't it?"

Dena shook her head. "Do you think Greg would mind if I use his office for a few minutes? I need to make a phone call."

"Oh, you go right ahead. He won't be in until after lunch. He had to drive over to Tahlequah this morning."

Dena went to the boss's office and sat at his desk for a moment to compose herself. She picked up the telephone and punched in her landlord's phone number. Harry Bosco answered after the fourth ring, his voice thick with sleep.

"Mr. Bosco, this is Dena Harris. I – "

"You again?"

"Yes, Mr. Bosco, me again. I have to get out of that house."

"Miss Harris, you signed a lease and like I told you yesterday, I will hold you to it in court if I have to. I don't care if you live there or not, you will pay the amount stated in the lease."

"Mr. Bosco, please," Dena said, fighting to keep the tears from her voice. "I can't stay there. I just can't. It's ... the house is ... Please, I just can't."

"Your lease is not negotiable, Miss Harris. Good-bye." He put his phone down, not bothering to do so gently.

Dena slowly returned her receiver to its cradle. She sat staring at the phone for a while, tears running down her face. She opened a drawer of Greg's desk and found a phone book. She looked up the number for The Benevolence Bugle and made another call.

"Can I speak to Robert Welch?" Dena asked the woman who answered. She was put on hold and a moment later Robert picked up the phone.

"Newsroom, this is Robert."

"Robert, it's Dena."

"Hi. How are you doing?"

"Not so good, actually. Listen, I wasn't honest with you the other night. About the house. It all sounded so ... so strange, you know? I mean, come on, a haunted house? I couldn't say I lived in a haunted house. That's just crazy. You know what I mean?"

"Dena, are you okay? You sound as if you're crying."

"I have been crying," Dena admitted. "Listen Robert, strange things have been happening. Bad things. I have to get out of there. I have to get my girls out. If I tell you everything and you write a story about it, do you think that asshole Harry Bosco will let me out of the lease just to shut me up?"

"Well, I don't know, Dena," Robert said. "Can't you just leave?"

"I don't have any money," Dena said. "We left last night and I floated a check at The Sleepy Pioneer motel. I have to ask my ex-husband for the money to cover that until payday. I need the deposit back from the house. I need my rent refunded so I can find someplace else to live. Someplace without voices and clothes flying across the room and … and … and shapes crouching over my baby."

""Shapes? Dena, that sounds bad. Real bad. I don't know if you'll get your money back, but we can try."

"Can we meet today? When will the story run?"

"Not today, Dena. God, I want to. I've wanted this for years, but it can't be today. I'm leaving in just a few minutes. I have to go to Oklahoma City to cover a meeting of the state transportation board. They're talking about building a new bridge over the river. It'll be tomorrow morning before I get back. Can it wait until then?"

"I … I don't know. Robert, I'm scared to go back."

"Well, Dena … Hey, how about if you stay at my place tonight. I won't be there."

"Could we? You wouldn't mind?"

"Please, Dena, do it."

"Thank you. I – " she stopped.

"Dena? Dena, what is it?"

"I can't. Danny's coming to town today. He's coming a day early to pick up the girls. He thinks he's sleeping on my couch tonight."

"Oh. Well, I don't know what to say. My offer stands, if you want it. In fact, I'll drop off my extra key with you on my way out of town. You do what you want. Okay?"

"Thank you, Robert. That's very sweet of you. I might let the bastard sleep there alone. Except … except the girls will want to be with him. They don't know why we don't live with him anymore."

"Yes, that's got to be hard on them."

"He's gay, you know," Dena said. "I never told anybody that before. Not even my own mother. Danny's gay. He didn't tell me that before he married me. Hell, he didn't tell me that until I was pregnant with Brianna. He said he didn't want to be gay, but he couldn't help it. He said he always pretended I was a man when we … when we had sex.

"I'm sorry. I shouldn't have dumped that on you," Dena said, wiping her eyes with her free hand, her other hand pressing the phone tight against her ear.

"No, Dena, that's fine. That's fine. Do you want me to see if someone else can cover for me today? Maybe we could just pick up the AP story."

"No. Really. I'm sorry, Robert. I'm doing bad enough at my job today, I don't want you to screw up yours. I'll be fine. I might well take you up on that offer to stay in your house tonight, though."

"I'll bring you the key."

"Thanks. I'll see you then."

Dena hung up the phone and went back to her own work area. Susan had cleaned up the spilled coffee and was retyping the ruined grant forms. "I'm really sorry about that," Dena said again.

"That's okay," Susan said, smiling up at her. "Did you get everything taken care of?"

"Oh, not really," Dena said. She sighed, the sigh threatening to become a sob. She smiled. "But I think it'll be okay." She went back to her file cabinets and began correcting her earlier mistakes.

A half-hour later, the office door opened and Robert

Welch came in wearing a sport coat and tie. Dena got up from her place beside a stack of folders on the floor and went to greet him, fighting the urge to throw her arms around his neck.

"Hi, Dena," he said, and she sensed that he, too, had the urge to make some kind of physical contact. His eyes flicked toward Susan, who sat watching the unfolding scene.

"Robert Welch, I swear you're hanging around here more and more since Dena got here," Susan said. "Is there anything I should know about?"

"She's just telling me all your dirty secrets, Susan," Robert joked. He returned his attention to Dena. "Had your morning break yet?"

"Well, I guess not …"

"Oh, go ahead," Susan said. She waved them away. "Just don't tell him *all* my secrets. Okay?"

"Thanks, Susan," Dena said. "And I promise not to tell him the one about the mailman." Susan's laughter followed them out the door.

"You okay?" Robert asked.

"Uh-huh. I guess."

"You don't look it. You look like someone who's survived a plane crash."

"Oh thanks," Dena said, laughing.

"Let's go to the café. I'll buy you some coffee and give you that key. Wouldn't Susan have loved it if I'd given you a key to my house right in front of her?"

"I'd never have heard the end of that one," Dena agreed.

The café was mostly deserted at mid-morning. They sat at a booth and both ordered coffee. "I really only have about fifteen minutes before I have to get out of town. Can you tell me in fifty words or less what's going on?" Robert asked, pushing a silver house key across the table as he did.

Dena took the key, turning it over and over in her hands as she thought about her answer. "Whispers," she said. "There are whispers. Screams. Howling. Shapes. Shapes made of shadow and … and blood. Not everything in the house wants to hurt us."

"What do you mean?"

"That guy who died in the bathtub. He … I saw him last night. I cut my leg while I was shaving and he … The blood became like a mist or something and it was shaped like a man and he said she wants my baby. He said Rosalyn Astor wants my baby. There's power in the blood, he said.

"Oh shit, Robert. You know how that sounds? It sounds crazy. But last night … last night she was in our bed. Robert, she was in our bed and she was crouching over Bree like some kind of animal. She slapped me off the bed. Bree was so cold. She was so cold, like ice, and I couldn't get her to wake up at first. I – I … I'm scared to go back."

"My God, Dena. My God."

"You believe me?"

"Of course I believe you."

The waitress appeared and left two cups of steaming coffee on the table. She cast a look at Dena's tear-stained face, then at Robert, her eyes accusing him of mistreatment before she spun on her heel and walked away.

"Dena, you can't go back there," Robert said. "You can't go back alone. Maybe not at all."

"Why me? What does she want from me?"

"This is just a guess, Dena, based on what I've read and what you've just told me. I think Rosalyn Astor wants to be alive again. I think she wants a living, flesh-and-blood body."

"What do you mean? What body?"

"I think she wants to possess your youngest daughter."

"Oh ..." Dena's hand flew to her mouth.

"That's just a guess. I don't know that. But, from what you've said that Brian Light told you and from what I've read in books about the occult, I'd say that's what she wants."

"What can I do?"

"Stay away. Dena, you have to stay out of that house."

Dena nodded, her hand dropping away from her mouth. Absently, she picked up her cup and sipped at her coffee, the ceramic rattling against her teeth.

"I have to go," Robert announced. "You stay at my house tonight. You and the girls. Even your ex, if you want. Nobody should be in that house." He paused, his eyes on Dena. She tried to smile at him and couldn't muster it. "Come on, I'll walk you back to your office," he said.

Robert threw some one-dollar bills on the table and they left. They parted at the door of her office and Dena watched him get into his car and drive away. She squeezed the silver key in her hand as she turned and went inside.

"Somebody is soooooo sweet on you," Susan said as the door closed behind Dena.

"I don't know," Dena said. "I think he's just a nice guy."

"Ha! That may be, but it doesn't change the fact he's got the hots for you."

"Oh, well … so what if he does?" Dena said, feeling her face redden. "I kind of like him, too."

Perhaps sensing that Dena needed company, Susan insisted they go to lunch together that day. They drove to the north edge of town and ate at the Western Sizzlin' steakhouse, both having salads. Susan pointed out different people in the restaurant and told stories about them.

"There's Alan Galusha," Susan said, pointing to an elderly, balding man sitting at a table with a woman who seemed to be his wife. "Oh, he's something. Been arrested twice for indecent exposure. As a kid, he used to hide in those bushes around the courthouse with some friends of his. They'd jerk off stray dogs, then push them onto the sidewalk when people passed by. Those dogs were so wound up they'd latch onto those people's legs and go to humping like there was no tomorrow."

"Oh, that is gross," Dena said, laughing so hard she almost dropped her fork.

She felt better for a while after lunch, until the phone rang and Susan handed the receiver to her. "It's for you."

"Hello?"

"Dena, it's me. Danny."

"Yeah."

"I just wanted to let you know I'm here. You should really keep your door locked."

"What?"

"Your front door. You should keep it locked. I just walked right in. Nice house."

"You're in the house?"

"Yes. What, you have some secret lover in here I'm not supposed to know about?"

"You shouldn't be in the house, Danny."

"Hey, I know, but I thought it would be okay. I mean, I'm not a stranger. I'm not going to steal anything. And the door wasn't locked."

"You shouldn't be in the house, Danny."

"You said that already."

"Danny …" Dena stopped. Robert was willing to believe the things that happened in the house. She knew Danny, however, would think she'd gone crazy. He might even use it as an excuse to reopen the custody battle over the girls. "Never mind."

"Hey, you want me to pick up the girls?"

"No. They won't let you do that. The daycare won't. They don't know you."

"The girls know me."

"Doesn't matter. They won't let the girls leave with you unless I sign a release form."

"Well, that's good of them, I guess. I can't believe you didn't tell them I might pick up the girls sometime."

"I just didn't think of it."

"Yeah. Whatever."

"I have to go, Danny. Make yourself comfortable there."

"All right. What time you get off?"

"Five. Bye." Dena hung up. "Shit."

"Bad news?" Susan asked.

"My ex-husband is in my house."

"You should call the cops."

"Probably," Dena said. She sighed and looked toward the clock; it was just after one. "Oh well. At least he didn't bring any friends with him."

Greg returned to the office a while later, beaming with excitement as he announced a partnership with the Main Street office in Tahlequah. "We're going to pool our resources and apply for money to build a hiking trail through the woods from Tahlequah to Benevolence. The transportation department might even kick in funds." He disappeared into his office and within moments Dena and Susan saw the light on their phone that indicated Greg was already making calls from his office.

"That'll keep him busy for a while," Susan said.

"Sounds like a big deal."

"Could be," Susan agreed. "Greg's an idea man. You'll learn that. He cooks them up, I apply for the money, and before the grant is rejected he's moved on to something else."

"Oh." Dena looked toward the boss's office, shrugged, and returned to her file folders.

The hours crawled across the face of the clock until finally, at ten minutes before five, Dena couldn't take it any longer. She asked if Susan would mind if she left early, then hurried out of the office with the other woman's blessing.

Dena picked up her daughters from the daycare and turned the car toward home.

"Your daddy is waiting for you," she said in a measured tone, her eyes finding Rebecca in the rearview mirror. She was disappointed by the look of excitement that lit up the girl's face.

"He is? Really?"

"Yes."

"He can keep the monsters away tonight," Rebecca

said.

"Did you tell anybody about what happened last night?" Dena asked.

"I tried, but Old Lady Witherspoon told me to stop trying to scare the other kids. She said I was making it up because they'd tried to scare me."

"Well, you shouldn't talk about it to other people, dumpling. They won't believe you. I doubt your daddy would believe it, either."

"You mean I can't tell Daddy?"

"I wish you wouldn't."

"But Mommy – "

"Please, dumpling? For me?"

She saw Rebecca sink back against the seat of the car, her arms crossed over her chest and her lower lip protruding. "I won't tell," the girl said.

"Thank you, sweetheart," Dena said.

She pulled the car into the driveway and killed the engine. The big white house that had looked so promising just days ago now loomed over the car, more menacing than a crouching cougar.

"I'll go in and get your father," Dena said. "He's taking us out to eat. You girls stay here."

Dena got out of the car and went to the front porch. The door was open a crack. Dena glanced back at the car and saw through the windows that Rebecca was reading a school book to Brianna. She pushed the door open and went inside.

"Danny?" Dena called when she didn't find her ex-husband sitting on the couch watching television. "Where are you?" She flicked a light switch, forgetting for a moment that all the bulbs had shattered the night before.

"Shit." She flipped the switch off and started through the living room, but froze in her tracks when she could look through the kitchen to the dining room.

Danny's body was sitting in a chair beside the dining table. His arms hung at his sides, pools of blood staining the carpet beneath each hand, wounds like laughing mouths gaping in both wrists.

"What do you want, Mommy? Is Daddy ready to go?"

Dena swung around and found Rebecca standing in the middle of the living room, holding Brianna by the hand.

"I told you to wait in the car," Dena said, her voice trembling. "What are you doing in here?"

"I heard you calling us," Rebecca answered. "You yelled at us to come inside and see Daddy. Where is he?"

"I ... I didn't call you," Dena said. "We have to get out of here."

Chapter 14

Dena hurried across the room and reached for Rebecca to spin her around and push her back toward the door. The girl saw her father sitting in the dining room, however, and ducked away from Rebecca to run to him. She stopped in the kitchen and began screaming. Dena grabbed Rebecca around the waist and lifted her up with one arm, reaching to cover her eyes with the other. She ran back to the living room, taking her hand off Rebecca's eyes to reach for Brianna's hand.

"Mommy! The door's gone!"

Dena looked away from Brianna to where Rebecca was pointing at the wall where the door had been a moment ago. It was no longer there. Dena looked around her. The windows were gone. She hurried to the wall where she knew a window was supposed to be and touched it with her hand. It felt solid. She moved around, touching where she knew there was no window. She could tell no difference. She went back to where the window had been and pounded, hoping to break through the illusion. Her hand was heavy and sounded dull as it slapped the paneled wall.

"Oh shit. Oh shit," Dena said, letting Rebecca slide out of her arms to stand on the floor beside her.

"Mommy? What do we do?"

"I don't know, Becky. I don't know," Dena said. She sank to the floor. Brianna came to her and Dena clutched the toddler tightly to her chest. She pulled Rebecca to her, pressing the girl's face against her own body so she couldn't turn her head and see the dead eyes of her father watching them from the other room.

"I have to check on Daddy," Dena said.

"I'll come, too."

"No, Becky, you won't. You will stay right here with your sister. Right where I can see you, but don't watch me, okay? Don't look. You just talk to Bree. Tell her what you did in school today. Okay."

"Is he dead, Mommy? Is Daddy dead?"

"I don't know, baby. That's what I'm going to find out." She sat Brianna on the floor. The girl tried to stand up, but Dena held her down.

"Becky's going to tell you a story," Dena said.

"No," Brianna answered. Rebecca reached to help Dena and Brianna pushed her away.

"It's okay, sweetie. Mommy will be right back. Here." Dena reached into her purse and took out a package of fruit snacks. She made sure Brianna saw them as she handed them to Rebecca. "Give her these one at a time."

"Canny?" Brianna asked.

"Yeah, it's candy," Rebecca promised.

Dena straightened and forced herself to approach the kitchen. As she crossed into the room she looked to the sink and saw that the window there was gone. She looked back to the unmoving form of her ex-husband, realizing that the big picture window in the wall behind him also was no longer there. *Where is the light coming from?* She didn't know, but she was thankful for it and doubted it would last past sunset.

Danny didn't move. His wide eyes were glassy and fixed, his mouth open, a trail of saliva dried in a streak from one corner. He was still dressed in his green army uniform; Dena's eyes lingered for a moment on the sergeant stripes, remembering how proud he was the day he earned them. Drops of blood fell from his fingers to the pools beneath him. A paring knife from Dena's kitchen drawer lay on one thigh, its blade smeared crimson.

Dena stretched out a trembling hand and touched the man's throat. The flesh was cool. There was no pulse.

"Oh God, Danny. Oh God."

A scratching sound came from somewhere to her right. Dena looked toward the basement door. The knob was moving. The scratching sound seemed to come from above the doorknob. Something knocked on the door as if with an old stick. Dena backed away until she was in the kitchen. *There's no way out of here. No doors, no windows.*

"Oh dear God, help me," she moaned. She reached out with both hands, her right coming in contact with something hard. She picked up a cast iron skillet from the stove and went back to the dining room. She closed her eyes for a moment, then threw open the door to the basement, jumping away as she did so.

A tall skeleton stood on the other side, its hand on the doorknob. As the door opened, the hand broke away from the wrist and fell to the floor, the finger bones scattering like so many dice. The skull turned on the spine so that the empty eye sockets faced Dena. The teeth parted, closed, parted again; crumbs of dirt fell from the mouth. More dirt clung to the bones and Dena thought of the cracks and little piles of soil she'd seen in the basement. *He was buried in the wall!*

Dena shrieked and threw the skillet. It crashed into the

rib cage, breaking bones and collapsing the figure in the doorway. The skull bounced on the carpet and rolled to a stop at Dena's feet, the eye sockets turned up.

Dena took a step back, bumped into the chair where Danny sat and jumped away. The sole of her shoe was slimed with blood and she slipped, landing hard on the floor behind Danny's body. Before she could get up, she saw the blood rising from the carpet just as it had done from her bath water the night before. Only this time there was much more of it and there were two shapes materializing before her.

The voice she'd heard from the blood-mist in the bathroom spoke to her. "She'll get stronger as you get weaker," it said.

Another voice Dena recognized from Robert's tape recorder spoke from the second cloud of red fog. "You have to destroy this body. She will use it. She – "

A scream of rage filled the house, shaking light fixtures and rattling dishes. A wind like the one Dena had felt that morning rushed into the dining room, swirling like a tornado, breaking up the misty figures made of spilled blood.

"Protect the baby," the voice of Brian Light said as his foggy form was torn apart.

Dena got to her feet and ran back to the living room. She threw herself at her daughters, pressing them to the wall, shielding them with her own body. Both girls were crying and clinging to her. Rebecca was begging to leave.

"I don't know how," Dena said. "I don't know how to get out. Oh shit, why didn't I do like Robert said. I never should have come back here."

"What are we going to do?"

"I don't know, Rebecca. Hush for a minute. Let me think. The telephone!" She jumped up and ran to the phone mounted on the wall beside the kitchen doorway. She picked up the receiver and put it to her ear. A loud squeal came from the device. She hung it up.

"It doesn't work?" Rebecca asked. Dena only shook her head. She started back toward her daughters. As she passed the entertainment center, she reached out and hit the power button of the television. To her surprise, the screen popped to life. She flipped to Nickelodeon and moved the girls to the couch to watch television.

"What about Daddy?" Rebecca asked.

"Daddy?" Brianna echoed.

"I'm sorry, honey. He's ... he is ... he's dead." Dena sank to her knees in front of the couch.

Rebecca's face crumbled and she began to cry harder than Dena had ever seen. "Oh baby, I'm so sorry." Dena reached for her daughter, but Rebecca recoiled. Then, to Dena's amazement, Rebecca slapped her hard across the face.

"It's your fault he's dead," Rebecca shouted. "If you hadn't left him and brought us here he wouldn't be dead. It's your fault. Your fault! I hate you!"

"Becky, I ... I ..."

Brianna was crying, probably because her sister was. Dena picked her up and hugged her tightly, stroking the girl's curly hair as her own tears wet the shoulder of Brianna's shirt. Dena's face stung from Rebecca's slap and she felt empty inside. The three of them cried for a while.

"Mommy? Mommy, I'm sorry," Rebecca said. "I'm sorry, Mommy."

Dena opened her arm and accepted Rebecca into her

embrace. "We can beat this thing," she said. "We can. We just have to keep our heads. We'll figure a way out of here."

"Really?"

"Uh-huh."

"How?"

"I'm not sure yet. But we'll think of something."

"I'm hungry."

Dena nodded and turned to Brianna, who was watching a cartoon. "Bree? Sweetie? Do you want to eat?"

"Eat!" Brianna agreed.

"Okay. I'm going to go to the kitchen and make something to eat," Dena said. "Mac and cheese okay with you two?" Rebecca nodded, so Dena stood up and went to the kitchen, forcing herself not to look at her dead ex-husband. *I have to take care of my girls. Nothing I can do for him now.*

She filled a pan with water and put it on the stove where the skillet had been. She tried not to think of the black skillet laying among the shards of a human skeleton just a few feet away. She turned the burner on the gas stove. The electronic igniter clicked once, twice, three times, four, then a cloud of blue flame burst from the burner, rising around the pan and reforming above it. For just a moment Dena was sure she saw the menacing face of a woman as the gas flames moved upward and died. She shook her head and looked at the pan of water. The burner was lit as normal under the pan.

As she waited for the water to boil, Dena stole into her bedroom and took the bedspread from the floor where it had fallen the night before. She went back to the dining room and quickly draped it over Danny's body, still sitting and staring vacantly in the chair.

She dumped pasta into the water, stirred it absently, listening to the cartoon playing in the other room. She remembered the days when cartoons had better characters than a sponge wearing square pants and living at the bottom of the sea. Dena drained the water, added the powdered cheese and stirred the pasta some more.

Are we really even going to try to eat a meal in this house? With … Danny's corpse sitting right there?

Her shoulders sagged and she paused in her stirring. A sob crawled up her throat, but she held it back. "I don't know what else to do," she whispered.

Dena dipped out three bowls and took them to the coffee table, then returned and took two cans of soda and Brianna's sipper cup of apple juice from the refrigerator. She went back to the living room and they began eating.

The cartoon broke for a series of commercials, the first of which was for a shampoo. That commercial faded to a blank screen. The television screen turned white, increasing in intensity until the living room was flooded with light. Then a woman's face – the same face Dena had just seen in the gas fire – appeared on the screen.

"She killed your daddy, just like my boy killed his daddy," the woman's face said, her dark eyes staring at Rebecca. "We don't need daddies." Her eyes moved to Brianna. "It's just us girls now."

Rebecca and Brianna were already screaming when Dena threw her bowl of macaroni and cheese at the television screen. The bowl shattered. Globs of sticky pasta clung to the screen like slugs.

"Get out of here!" Dena screamed. The woman was laughing, her dark eyes filled with black light, her wild, disheveled hair flying around her face. Then the face faded away and was replaced by the cartoon, already in progress.

"Who is she, Mommy?"

"She's a witch who used to live here," Dena said. "She's dead. A ghost."

"A ghost-witch?"

"Yes."

"Like in Scooby Doo?"

"No, baby, not like Scooby Doo," Dena said. She turned off the television, which further upset Brianna now that the cartoon was back on the screen. "You two just eat. Okay?"

Dena let her mind race with possibilities as she cajoled Brianna to eat. She considered setting a fire in the back of the house in hopes the neighbors would see it and call the fire department. *But what if they don't see it? What if all the smoke is trapped inside and we can't get out?*

She felt sure the missing doors and windows was nothing more than an illusion cast by the witch-ghost, as Rebecca called her, but Dena couldn't think of a way to dispel the illusion. She knew where the doors and windows were supposed to be, but she couldn't find them.

What if we can never get out? What does she want?

She remembered Robert's theory that she wanted to be flesh again. The ghost of Brian Light had warned her again to guard Brianna. Would Rosalyn try to possess the toddler? *Why Brianna? How?* Dena had no answers.

A new thought came to her. She turned over the feeding duties to Rebecca and went to her bedroom where she rummaged through an unpacked box until she found a Bible with a blue cover. She returned to the living room and sat between her daughters. She opened the book and began thumbing through the pages.

A low grumble rolled through the house. It was like the warning growl of a lion. Dena couldn't help a small smile of triumph. At last she'd found something the ghost-witch didn't like. She found the Psalms and began to read.

The wind that had twice before passed through the house came again, this time focused on the book in Dena's hands, trying to wrench it from her grasp. Dena clung to the Bible her father had given her years before. The pages fluttered around her fingers. Rebecca and Brianna were hanging onto her and screaming again. Dena laughed.

"You don't like this, do you bitch?" she yelled. "I've got you now. I've got you now, you bitch!" She laughed harder.

Rebecca's scream rose to a higher pitch. The focus of the wind shifted from the Bible in Dena's hands to her older daughter. Rebecca was torn away from her mother. She hovered in the air over the couch for a moment, her arms and legs flailing, a look of total terror on her face.

"Okay, okay!" Dena dropped the book onto the coffee table.

Rebecca fell onto the couch, bounced and slipped onto the floor. Dena grabbed her daughter and pulled the child onto her lap.

The Bible rose from the table and exploded like a paper bomb, sending fragments of Holy Scripture fluttering around the room like so much confetti. Rosalyn Astor's demonic laughter filled the house, cackling on for several moments before fading away.

The house became quiet except for sobs. The three females on the couch sat pressed together, quiet for the most part, but occasionally crying again. The room darkened as an unseen sun sank behind a hidden horizon somewhere in the sane world outside the house.

"We have to stay awake," Dena said. "She is stronger when we're asleep. She always does something when we're asleep. We have to stay awake."

"I think Brianna is already asleep," Rebecca said.

Dena looked at the youngest of the two girls curled on either side of her. Brianna was asleep, her blue eyes closed, her red lips slightly parted. She was breathing heavily. "That's okay," Dena said. "One of us should stay awake, though, so we can wake up the other one if something happens."

"Do you want to go to sleep first?"

"No, baby, I want you to go to sleep," Dena said. "When I can't stay awake any longer, I'll wake you up. I'll try to think of something for you to do while you're on guard duty. Okay?"

"I can watch TV."

"No, I don't think so. She can control that."

"Okay, Mommy. I'll try to sleep."

Dena was surprised at how easily Rebecca slipped into slumber. In no time, the girl was breathing deeply, her body much heavier where it pressed against her mother. Dena leaned her head back, pushing it into the cushioned sofa. Her eyes rolled to the ceiling. She had no idea if the witch's spell would break in the morning. She had no reason to suspect it would. She had no idea how long she and the girls could hold out against the evil ghost.

She felt her eyelids drooping and forced them up. They threatened to close again. She willed them open, staring zombie-like at the wall across from her. Slowly, her eyes rolled up, her chin sagged and her eyelids came down.

"I'm sorry, Dena," Danny said. "I gave her what she needs. I shouldn't have come here. I shouldn't have married you when I knew all along what I was. I brought this on you and my girls. I'm sorry, Dena."

Dena tried to rouse herself. *Am I dreaming? Is Danny still alive? What's he talking about?* She couldn't drag herself back to consciousness.

"You have to do something about my body, Dena. You have to cut off my penis. If you don't, she'll use it on Bree. She has to so she can possess her. Dena, do you hear me?"

Dena groaned.

"Dena, she's coming back. I can't stay. She's too strong. The son, Matt Junior, he says she'll be weakest when she's in my body. You have to ..."

"Danny!" Dena started up on the couch. The walls around her were shaking under a tremendous booming, as if they were being pounded by giant fists. Dena put her arms around her girls again and hugged them tighter.

The booming stopped abruptly. The house was quiet.

"He's a liar and a fag and he's dead now. Dead by his own hand." The woman's voice was a hissing whisper that filled the room and made Dena's hair stand on end.

Quiet. Silence. Dena stared ahead of her. She looked to her right and to her left. She saw a shape in the dining room and jerked involuntarily. She convinced herself it was not the same shape she'd seen in her bed the night before. It was only Danny's covered corpse. Poor Danny, she thought.

"*...destroy the body ... cut off the penis ... possess Bree ...*"

The warnings came back to her. Two ghosts now had warned her to destroy the body of her ex-husband. *Or was*

Danny's ghost just a dream? Dena didn't know. She struggled with the thought of mutilating her ex-husband's body. *The police will think I killed him.*

Painfully, time crept by. Dena had no idea what the hour was. Her girls slept soundly beside her. The house remained quiet. After a long inner struggle, Dena came to the conclusion she couldn't risk ignoring the warnings. She untwined herself from her daughters and got to her feet. She started for the kitchen, running over in her mind where the sharpest of her butcher knives was and how she would know it in the dark.

As she neared the kitchen doorway, the bulbless light fixtures in the downstairs area suddenly came to life, quickly crescendoing to blinding brilliance. The telephone rang, one prolonged, ear-splitting ring. Dena looked to the machine in time to see the receiver fly from its place on the wall. It slammed into her forehead and bounced away.

Dena felt her knees buckling. As if in slow motion, she could feel her body folding up from the bottom and she drifted toward the floor as her eyes rolled up so she could see nothing but the blackness inside her skull.

Steven E. Wedel

DAY SEVEN

Chapter 15

"Mommy. Mommy. Mommy, wake up."

Dena forced her eyelids to open and rolled her eyeballs down to find the source of the voice. Her head ached incredibly and her vision swam, refusing to come into focus. She could hear Rebecca talking to her, but she couldn't concentrate to hear the words. *Where is Brianna? Why can't I hear Brianna?* She closed her eyes for a moment, took a deep breath and opened them again.

"Mommy, the skelegan head wants to talk to you."

"Umm?" Dena realized she was still laying on her side on the living room floor. Her eyes were on a level with Rebecca's bare feet. "What did you – " Her voice stuck in her throat. She sat up and backed away quickly. "Put that down!"

Rebecca was holding the skull from the skeleton that had been scratching at the basement door. At her mother's order, the girl bent and gently placed the skull on the floor between herself and Dena.

"He wants to talk to you," Rebecca said.

"Wh - who does?" Dena asked.

"The skelegan head." Rebecca pointed to the skull.

"It talked to you?"

"Yes. It was hollering from in the dining area after the phone hit you. I couldn't wake you up, so I went to see who was hollering. He said he can help us."

Dena looked from her daughter's face to the fleshless head resting on the carpet.

"Go ahead, Mr. Skelegan," Rebecca urged. "Talk to her."

"I am Matthew Astor," a voice said.

Dena felt a scream rising from her bowels. The voice was coming from the skull, although its jaw didn't move. She moaned and backed further away. "Come here," she commanded Rebecca. The girl stepped over the skull and came to stand beside Dena. "Where's your sister?"

"She's still sleeping on the couch," Rebecca said. Dena looked and saw a dark shape she recognized as her youngest daughter curled up in a corner of the sofa.

"Listen to me," the skull demanded. "Time is running out. She is coming. She is draining the life force from your daughter right now. She is getting stronger. Soon, she will come for the girl."

"How can you ...?" Dena could only stare at the talking skull.

"Before she made our son kill me, my sister bound my soul to my body, even in death. They buried me under the house. That is of no consequence now. She will take the body of the man who died yesterday. She will use that male body to kill the child and implant her own soul in the child's body."

"No, no, no," Dena argued. "Danny would never – "

"She has driven away the others," the skull interrupted. "Our son, the man who died in the bathtub and the one you call Danny. She has banished them so that they cannot interfere with her again. She is powerful. She is gathering her strength to use the body of the man. His will was weak. She convinced him to kill himself so she could use him."

"What can I do?"

"Destroy the body," the skull said.

"Nooooo," Dena protested. "Not Danny ..."

"He is dead. What you see is a husk of flesh that is of no consequence to the soul that has departed it. However, if you value your daughter's life, you will destroy the husk."

"Why are you telling me this?"

"I helped her in life. In my years of captive death I have done nothing but think of how she betrayed me. Your escape will be my retribution. Your salvation will be mine."

From the gloom of the kitchen two hands reached out and closed around the skull, raising it into the air. Dena's eyes followed the ascending skull until it stopped on a level with the face of her dead husband. Danny's eyes glowed in the diminishing dimness of the house.

"No salvation for you, my love." The voice that came from Danny's mouth was female, filled with hate ... the same voice from the tape recorder, from Dena's dreams, from the television. Danny's hands brought the skull closer until his dead lips were pressed against the bare teeth in a brutal kiss.

"Wake the child," the voice of the skull said.

The force controlling Danny roared with rage. His hands came together, turning the skull into an explosion of gray dust. The particles floated toward the floor and the voice of Matthew Astor was heard no more. Danny's glowing eyes fixed on Dena.

"Hide, Becky, hide," Dena screamed. She shoved Rebecca away and scrambled toward the couch and her youngest daughter. Rebecca shrieked and ran to the bathroom, slamming the door behind her. Dena heard the click of the lock just as she grabbed Brianna from the cushions.

"Wake up, sweetie, wake up," Dena said, shaking her daughter, trying to be gentle but forceful. "Come on, Bree, wake up for Mommy. Wake up, Bree! Wake up right now!"

Danny was advancing on her, his hands at his side, his eyes blazing, his jaw hanging open while the demonic laughter of Rosalyn Astor spilled from somewhere inside him. He came forward slowly, steadily, confident that she could not escape. Dena backed away, clutching Brianna to her chest, shaking her and begging her to wake up.

"You know what I'm going to do to her, bitch?" the woman's voice asked from Danny's corpse. "I'm going to kill her. And then I'm going to fuck her. Then I will become her. I will be your daughter. Will you be my mommy? Will you hold me like you hold her now?"

"Stop it! Stop it! Stop it!" Dena screamed. Her back was to the wall. She scooted along the paneled wall until she was trapped in a corner with nothing but a cheap rocking chair between her and the monster inside her dead ex-husband's body. "Wake up, Brianna, wake up," she cried. "For God's sake, wake up."

"Shut up, you cunt," the woman yelled. Danny's hands lifted the rocker and flung it aside. The hands reached for Dena, reached for the child she held. Dena dropped to the floor and turned away, hunching her body over Brianna's, pressing the toddler between herself and the wall. She felt Danny's hand in her hair, clutching, pulling her head back. She saw a seam in the paneling, then her head slammed into the wall and she blacked out again.

Chapter 16

The next time Dena awoke, the house was filled with light. She was still in the corner of the living room, fragments of the broken rocking chair littering the carpet around her. She looked toward the nearest window, saw it still wasn't visible, despite the light in the house, then realized Brianna was no longer in her arms.

"Brianna!" she yelled, jumping to her feet and spinning around. The sudden movement made her woozy. She reached out and steadied herself against the walls. Her eyes fixed on something yellowish-white laying on the tan carpet. Slowly she understood it was Brianna's diaper, swollen with urine. The toddler's torn clothes lay not far away. "Bree!" Dena screamed.

She didn't have to look far to find her youngest daughter. Her eye caught motion from the dining room. She focused her eyes through the pain pulsing in her head and saw Danny's possessed form beside the table. He was naked. His arms were raised, but all Dena could really see was his bare back, buttocks and the backs of his legs. She took a few shaky steps, found that she could walk, and moved faster toward the kitchen and the dining room beyond.

"Bree!" she shouted again.

"Mommy?" Rebecca called from the bathroom. Dena paused and looked toward the closed door.

"Stay in there, Rebecca," she ordered. "Keep that door locked."

"Okay, Mommy."

Dena entered the kitchen. Danny's head was back, his empty, burning eyes toward the ceiling as strange words spilled from his mouth in a feminine voice. Dena kept moving until the counter dividing the kitchen from the dining room was close enough she could see over it to the dining room table.

Brianna was laying on the table, her small body stripped of all clothing, her arms and legs splayed so that she looked like a pale, stranded starfish. Dena's own emergency candles were placed around Brianna's head, providing unneeded illumination. The girl still slept heavily. Dena nearly fainted with relief as she saw the girl's chest rising and falling with deep breaths. Dena's best butcher knife lay on the table beside her daughter, its blade reflecting the small flames of the candles.

The female voice droned on from Danny's mouth. Dena's eyes traveled from the face down the torso and stopped when she came to the engorged penis pointing like an accusatory sausage over the top of the table ... pointing at Brianna.

... *Reborn* ...

The conversation with the ghost of Brian Light came back to her, reminding her of the witch's intent.

"No!" Dena dove forward and grabbed the handle of the butcher knife. Rosalyn's voice roared from Danny's mouth as Dena plunged the blade toward his groin. She missed, raking the point across his thigh as the body was moved away from her. A fist slammed into her jaw. Dena staggered away, fearing she would black out again, knowing she would never be able to help Brianna if she lost consciousness again. Black waves slammed into her, but she fought to stay on her feet.

"Dena! Dena!" The voice was accompanied by thunderous pounding from somewhere behind her.

Dena tried to look toward the new sound, but Danny's corpse was advancing on her. She concentrated all her energy on backing away, the knife held before her, a streak of blood running down the blade.

Danny lunged. Dena slashed and fell back. She saw a new wound open across the back of his right hand. His dead blood filled the gash, thick and dark, but did not spill out. Rosalyn laughed at her.

"Dena! Open the door!"

That's Robert Welch!

"I can't find it," Dena screamed. "Help me!"

"I'm coming in," Robert yelled from somewhere outside.

Dena darted forward, slashing again at Danny's penis. His left fist came down on her right shoulder, almost driving her to the ground. She stumbled backward, desperate to keep hold of the knife. *Hurry, Robert, hurry!*

Something struck the wall behind her – something harder than a knocking hand. Danny's burning eyes left her face for a moment, looking over Dena's shoulder. Dena dared a quick look behind her and saw the head of an axe being pulled out of the door.

The door! I can see the door!

The axe struck again. The knob fell off and the door shuttered open. Robert stood on the other side, wearing jeans and a polo shirt, an axe with a plastic yellow handle held in both hands.

"Get out!" Rosalyn screeched.

Danny's body lurched forward, grabbing Dena and

flinging her aside, ignoring the new cut she managed to inflict in his abdomen. Dena crashed into a glider rocker, knocking it over and falling on top of it. The wooden arm slammed into her back. She was sure she felt a rib break.

"Kill it, Robert. Kill it," she wailed. "It's Rosalyn Astor."

Dena rolled off the chair in time to see Robert step through the doorway, the axe raised above his head as he closed with Danny's possessed body. Danny dove at him. Robert brought the axe down, burying the blade in Danny's skull, forcing the body to the carpet. He jerked the blade free.

Danny's body never hesitated, but got to its feet again and rushed at Robert, arms extended, eyes blazing, a snarl rolling from his mouth.

"Holy fucking shit," Robert said as he danced away from the body. He swung the axe again, like slicing with a sword, and planted the head in Danny's side. The body stumbled but never paused.

Before Robert could pull the blade free, Danny's hands were on his throat, pushing him back against the wall. Robert had to let go of the axe and struggle to get the hands off his throat.

"Mommy, what's happening?" Rebecca yelled from the bathroom.

"Becky!" Dena called. The bathroom door opened and Rebecca peeked out. Dena put her hands under her and pushed up, trying to get to her feet. Blinding pain stabbed through her from her side. Her vision darkened again. "Dammit! I will not pass out," she vowed.

"Mommy, Mommy, what's Daddy doing?" Becky was beside Dena pointing to the naked body of her father.

Dena was on her knees. She grabbed Rebecca's shoulders. "Your sister is on the dining room table. Asleep. Wake her up. Throw water on her, whatever it takes. You have to wake her up. Go!" She shoved Rebecca toward the kitchen.

Dena found her dropped knife and used the arm of the couch to push herself to her feet. She went after her ex-husband.

The spirit possessing Danny was so intent on choking the life from Robert that Dena wasn't noticed as she approached. She reached around the corpse with both arms, grabbing the swollen penis in her left hand and bringing up the blade of the knife with her right.

As soon as the cold steel touched the body, Rosalyn dropped Robert and turned Danny on his ex-wife. He spun around, bringing up an elbow and slamming it into Dena's chest. She stumbled back, dragging the knife along his hip and opening another useless wound.

"I'm tired of playing with you, bitch," Rosalyn said. "I thought it would be fun to keep you and make you take care of me in your little girl's body, but I've decided you should die."

Danny came after her, the axe still buried in his side, the handle sticking out like a withered third arm. Dena backed away, the knife held before her. Then, for no apparent reason, the corpse stumbled. The light in the eyes flickered and dulled, but did not go out. A moment later Dena heard Rebecca.

"Mommy, she's awake, but she keeps trying to go back to sleep."

Dena looked behind her and saw Rebecca standing in the doorway to the kitchen, Brianna in her arms. The toddler had her arms and legs wrapped around her big sister, her head resting on Rebecca's shoulder. Brianna's eyes drooped and closed.

"Put her back!" Rosalyn shrieked. She moved Danny's body toward the girls.

"No you don't!" Dena jumped between the corpse and her daughters.

Danny's body never hesitated. The light of his eyes increased in intensity as he moved ... as Brianna drifted back to sleep.

Dena saw Robert launch himself at the body. He wrapped his arms around Danny's neck and shoulder, tackling him. Both men fell to the floor. Robert grabbed the axe handle and began pulling. Danny also grabbed it and held firmly, keeping the blade in his side to keep the weapon away from his attacker.

Seeing her chance, Dena fell on Danny. As Rosalyn used Danny's hands to keep the axe away from Robert, Dena grabbed the penis again. This time she was quicker, her aim true. The appendage came off cleanly in her hand.

An explosion of thunder came from Danny's body. The house shook. Robert fell away from the body, the axe tearing away and dropping beside him. Dena jumped away, moving toward her girls; both of them were crying for her now.

Danny's body ceased all motion except for a trembling that shook him from head to foot. Dena watched, horrified, as her ex-husband's body ripped open like a busting seam on a teddy bear, the rip originating from his crotch. A sound like a scream came from the opening. Then, a black shape, darker than midnight, denser than old engine oil, rose from Danny's scrotum. The black shape took the form of a woman, hovering, undulating, writhing in the air above the body. A moaning sound rolled from the shape, wrapped around it, became an agonized scream.

The black shape exploded and vanished, leaving nothing but the smell of burned ozone behind her.

"Oh. My. God," Robert whispered.

"Mommy, she wants you."

Dena forced herself to look away from the ruined body of the man she'd married and divorced. She round Rebecca, her face pale and streaked with tears, barely holding onto Brianna as the younger girl fought to get down, her arms stretched toward her mother as she cried.

"My babies," Dena said, running to them and throwing her arms around both of them.

"Mommy, I don't want to live here anymore," Rebecca said.

"Oh, honey, we are getting out of here today," Dena promised. "This is our last day in Benevolence."

ABOUT THE AUTHOR

Steven E. Wedel lives in central Oklahoma with his wife and most of his kids ... the ones who haven't grown up enough to leave the den yet, anyway. He began writing in the mid-1980s and has kept at it despite numerous disappointments and setbacks. Steve has a bachelor's degree in journalism from the University of Central Oklahoma and a master's degree in liberal studies from the University of Oklahoma. He has worked as a machinist, bookseller, stock clerk, journalist, public relations specialist and is now a high school English teacher most of the year.

Visit him online at www.stevenewedel.com.